Saving Cassie

Stone Knight's MC
Book 2

Megan Fall

Saving Cassie
Published by Megan Fall

Dedication

To my mother
Jeanne
Who has always been my biggest supporter!

Contents

Chapter One
Cassie

Cassie cried out as she fell to the floor. The hit was hard, but she knew it wasn't hard enough to draw blood. Parker knew how much strength to use when he hit her, so it wouldn't leave a mark. Heaven forbid he left a bruise that she couldn't cover up. If he marked her face, he always made sure she iced the area thoroughly, to prevent it from swelling.

She stayed on the ground so she didn't provoke him further and kept her eyes on the floor. Tonight he was in a good mood, so he huffed and stomped away. She stayed where she was and waited until she heard the bedroom door slam. Seconds later it came, and she breathed a sigh of relief.

She pushed herself up carefully and made her way to the kitchen. She opened the freezer and pulled out her trusty bag of peas. She knew it was a night she needed them. After a year of abuse, she could just tell.

She made her way back to the couch and plopped down. Gently, she lifted the peas and placed them on her cheek. She winced at the cold, but then moaned in relief as the pain slowly subsided. Tomorrow would be a good day, the swelling would be minimal and the bruising would be light enough to cover with a bit of makeup. She sighed, knowing she got off lucky tonight.

She thought back to when she first met Parker. Her parents were incredibly strict and raised her with almost no freedom. She had to dress a certain way, she had to act a certain way, and she could only be friends with a certain type of people.

Her life had been hard growing up. Her father was a partner in a huge law firm and never had time for her. Her mother was a socialite, and there were a dozen charities and functions she needed to attend. Her parents were never home, and Cassie relished the time alone. She could breathe when they weren't around, and she didn't have to worry about being the perfect daughter.

She went on lots of dates, her parents made sure of that. Unfortunately, she hated all the boys, then later men, her parents insisted on setting her up with. They were boring, stuck up rich kids, who were only out to suck up to her father. They knew a marriage to her was a full ride in his prestigious law firm. They didn't care about her, they cared about the status she would bring and the money they would earn.

That's how she met Parker. Her parents forced her to go on yet another date. If she wanted to stay in their house, she had to follow their rules. She had gotten ready for the date the same way she had for all the others, but when the doorbell rang and she got a look at him, her heart fluttered. He was taller than most of the men her parents set her up with. He had short blonde hair and the most beautiful blue eyes. He wasn't dressed in a suit, like the rest usually were. Instead, he wore jeans and a button up dress shirt. When he smiled at her, she couldn't help but smile back.

He showed her the attention and love she had been craving from her parents. They dated for two years before he proposed. At twenty two, she thought she loved him. He took her for romantic dinners, he bought her expensive gifts and he seemed to put her before her parents.

He was a dream come true, and she was smitten. Unfortunately, once they were married, he showed his true colours. On their wedding night, he sat her down and explained how it was going to be. She was to act to the part of the doting wife and he would be discreet about the other women he was sleeping with. She was to stay home, cooking the meals and keeping the house, while he went out drinking with the boys and sleeping with whoever caught his attention that week.

Her life turned upside down in a minute, and not for the better. She learned her place quickly, because if she didn't, there would be repercussions. Tonight was just a small one, all because she asked how his day went.

Chapter Two
Steele

Steele was on the worst date of his life. He knew his standards were pretty low, but this was ridiculous. He usually went to a bar, picked up a girl, went back to her place, and then left before she fell asleep. Recently, his best friend Jaxon had gotten hitched. Now, he lived in a quiet little cabin by a lake and he was expecting a daughter in a couple months. And, the man was incredibly happy.

Steele figured it was time for him to find someone of his own. He wanted everything Jaxon had, and at twenty-eight, he was ready. This was why he was sitting in a restaurant right now. If he wanted a woman, he need to get to know one. That meant he needed to go on dates.

His current date was pretty enough, tall, with long black hair and a rocking body, but that was all she had going for her. When she laughed, it sounded like a hen cackling, and she laughed a lot. She also talked a lot although he couldn't tell you one thing she said. He wasn't even listening anymore, but she just kept going. Since she didn't stop he figured he was doing okay, nodding whenever she paused for a minute.

He had brought her to a nice steak place, and he had ordered a steak and a beer. She ordered a salad and a glass of wine. With no food or any substance in her stomach, the wine was starting to get to her. She was beginning to get handsy, and he was ready to walk out.

He was turning to tell her exactly that when the hostess brought a couple to the table beside theirs. The man was impeccably dressed and looked to be well off. It was the woman he was with that caught his attention.

She was tiny, probably only about five foot two, and had gorgeous long blonde hair. She wore a pretty summer dress and had on low heals. He was instantly taken by her. He had never felt this drawn to someone before, and it was a little unnerving. She sat down beside the man and kept her head down.

The man was holding up a menu and Steele noticed a wedding ring on his hand. Of course, the woman would be married. The husband said something to her, and she lifted her head to answer, catching Steele's eyes. Their gazes locked for a minute and she seemed frozen. Slowly, a small, timid smile appeared on her lips, and Steele grinned back. She flushed red, but didn't look away.

Then she cried out and turned to her husband. Steele saw he had grabbed her arm and was speaking harshly to her. She nodded and dropped her head back to the table. When the husband let her go, her arm was red where he had held it. The man turned and glared at Steele, and Steele calmly smirked back.

Finally, the man looked away as his waitress appeared and his attention was drawn to her.

The woman glanced up for a second to look at Steele again, and then her eyes darted back to the table. It was a brief moment, but it was long enough for Steele to see a tear in the woman's eye.

His blood ran cold. Maybe it was a one-time thing, and the husband was just having a bad day. He certainly hoped so. He turned back to see his date was still chatting away and picking at her salad. She hadn't even noticed that his attention had been on the other table.

Instead of leaving, Steele decided he really wanted to finish his steak, and maybe order desert. He kept his eye on the couple even though it was really none of his business. Twice more, the husband grabbed her harshly then leaned down to say something in her ear.

She never looked at Steele again until she was leaving. When the husband stood and headed for the exit, she followed dutifully behind him. When she was almost to the door, she turned back and took a last look back. Steele held her eyes. He could see the sadness there, then she turned and walked out the door.

Steele knew, if that woman hadn't been married, she would have been leaving with him instead.

Chapter Three
Cassie

Cassie nervously watched Parker as he pulled into the driveway. He radiated anger, and it made her cringe. His anger always meant bad things for her. He parked and got out of the car, slamming his door as he headed for the house. Cassie slowly got out and trailed behind him.

He unlocked the front door and motioned for her to go in ahead of him. Head down, she stepped inside and he followed, slamming that door too. She cried out as he suddenly grabbed her arm, spinning her around and slamming her back into the front door. He pinned her body to the door with his.

She refused to look up at Parker and kept her eyes on his chest. He was tall and lean, spending hours playing tennis and golf. Roughly, he grabbed her chin and forced her head up.

"Do you enjoy disrespecting me," he calmly asked her. "Because a happily married woman never looks at another man the way you did tonight. And he was a biker and a criminal," he spat. "That's scraping the bottom of the barrel darling. I have my mistresses, but I never flaunt them in front of you." He leaned in close, "if I ever catch you looking at another man the way you did tonight, I will end you."

Then, he released her chin, and she thought that was it, but his hand shot to the top of her head and grabbed a huge chunk of her hair. Cassie cried out and threw her hands up trying to pull his away. She was no match for him, and she screamed when he yanked her head forward, then slammed it hard against the steel door.

The pain from the hit was excruciating and when he let go, she slid to the floor. Black spots appeared behind her eyes and she leaned forward, breathing in and out until they went away. She felt the back of her head and already there was a lump forming. Her hand came away sticky, and she cringed wondering how she was going to clean it.

He leaned over her and locked the door. As he walked away, he suddenly stopped and looked back at her. "Remember who you belong to darling," he ordered. She watched as he grabbed a bottle of bourbon from the liquor cabinet and headed up to the bedroom.

Carefully, she pushed herself off the floor and headed to the spare bathroom. She grabbed a towel and held it to the back of her head. When she pulled it away it was covered in quite a bit of blood. She probably needed stitches, but she knew Parker wouldn't let her see a doctor. That meant people might find out that he hurt her, and he wanted it kept a secret.

Cassie sat on the bath mat and pulled her knees up to her chest. She rested her forehead on them and closed her eyes and put the towel back on her head. After a few minutes, and a look at the towel, she realized the bleeding had stopped. She threw the towel on the corner and started the shower.

Parker pretty much hated her now, so when he started sleeping around she moved her things into the spare room. It had become her sanctuary. He rarely had sex with her anymore, and she was grateful for that. She never enjoyed it, and it always hurt. He had started to hit her a lot lately, but it was never as bad as tonight.

She climbed under the spray and gently washed her hair. When she was done, she patted it dry and slipped on her bathrobe. She left the bathroom and padded to the kitchen barefoot. She grabbed a glass of water and took a couple of painkillers, then filled a bag with ice. Cassie went into the living room and plopped down on the couch.

As she fell asleep there, with the ice on her head, she dreamed of the handsome biker from the restaurant. She knew a dream was all he would ever be.

Chapter Four
Cassie

Two days later Cassie found herself driving down a county road. She just needed a break, so she had hopped in her car, rolled down the windows and headed for the outskirts of town. She had a headache that wouldn't go away, and she still had a fairly large lump at the back of her head. Luckily, it had only bled once more since the other night. She had thrown on some sunglasses, hoping it would help the headache.

Cassie loved the back roads. It was quiet and peaceful out here. She tried to lose herself in them, forgetting her problems for a little while.

Life just wasn't turning out the way she thought it would. She needed to step away for a couple hours.

Cassie saw some horses up ahead and decided to stop. She carefully pulled off the paved road, and on the soft gravel shoulder. As she got out of the car, a couple horses whinnied and headed towards her. She smiled happily as she stepped up on the bottom rung of the fence.

When the horses got close, they stopped and stuck their heads over the fence. She laughed and jumped down, not wanted to be knocked off. She was short, standing on the ground, but the horses just leaned down and huffed at her.

She moved closer and held out her hand. A beautiful chestnut horse sniffed her hand, then nudged it with his head. She took the hint and scratched him on the top of his head. She had no idea how long she stood there petting the horses, but she figured she should move on.

Reluctantly, she got in her car and started it up. As she was easing back onto the road, she heard something scraping on the ground.

Sighing, she manoeuvred back onto the shoulder. She got out and moved to the back of the car where she thought the noise was coming from.

As she was bending down to see under the car, a loud rumbling noise caught her attention. She quickly stood back up and looked down the road. Four motorcycles were headed her way. Cassie froze, not knowing what to do. If she jumped in her car, it would look like she was afraid of them. She was though, being all alone and stuck as she was.

As the motorcycles got closer, the one in the front pointed at her and they all pulled up behind her car. Nervously, she watched as they shut down their bikes and got off. Four huge, muscled, scary looking men headed towards her.

"Can we help you sweetheart," the one closest to her asked. Putting up a brave front, she looked up towards them. One biker in particular caught her eyes, and she gasped as he smirked at her. She took a small step back as she realized he was the biker from the restaurant the other night.

"Is there something wrong with your car," the other biker asked again.

She swung her eyes back to him and shyly said, "it sounds like something is dragging on the ground."

"Trike, take a look," he ordered. One of the other bikers ran ahead and crouched down to look under her car.

When the biker from the other night stepped forward, she nervously looked up at him. Without a word, he gently took her arm and pushed the short sleeve of her dress up. She squirmed and tried to pull away, but it was too late. His eyes darkened as he looked at the bruise on arm.

"He hurt you," the beautiful biker growled. She looked away from him, and this time when she pulled at her arm, he let her go.

The biker that had looked under her car explained that she had lost one of the clamps that held the muffler on. If it wasn't fixed right away, she could lose the muffler altogether.

"Our clubhouse is just down this road, and we have a repair shop," the first biker said. "Follow us there and it will only take a minute to get you fixed up."

She looked back at the biker from the restaurant and then made a split second decision that she prayed was the right one.

She nodded, looking directly at the biker she dreamed of.

Chapter Five
Steele

Steele watched as the woman got into her car, then he followed his brothers back to his hog. When he was seated and ready to start it up, he caught Dagger's eye.

"Some fucker hurt her," he commented. All of his brothers had a zero tolerance for violence against woman, but Dagger felt the strongest. Steele figured something might have gone down in his past to make him that way, but Dagger wouldn't say.

"Saw her at a restaurant the other day," Steele told him. "Husband grabbed her arm a couple times. Looked like he was pretty rough. Two days later, the bruise is still there."

Dagger nodded. "Anything between you two," he asked.

"Just saw her at the restaurant, didn't even talk to her," he stated. "Don't even know her name."

"Pretty heavy eye contact brother. That happened at the restaurant too," he questioned.

"Think it's the reason the husband grabbed her," he answered. "And before you ask, yes I'm interested, but she's married brother." Then he cranked the throttle and headed down the road. He heard his brothers follow, then a quick glance in the rear-view mirror showed the woman had pulled out behind them.

One of the brothers opened the gate when he saw them coming and they rolled through. Steele headed to the garage, and pulled up in front, while his brothers headed to the clubhouse. He nodded his thanks that they left him to handle this. He powered down the bike and climbed off, motioning the woman to pull into the bay.

Once she was in position, he strode over and opened her door. She seemed surprised and a bit unsure, but she got out. As she stood beside him, he noticed how fucking small she was. She barely cleared the middle of his chest. Most of the women he dated were taller, and he was shocked to see he enjoyed the height difference.

"Hey Little Mouse," he started. "Go hang in that chair beside the bench for a minute while I take a look."

She looked up at him. "Little Mouse," she asked.

"Don't know your name, but you're tiny and quiet and a bit skittish. So, Little Mouse."

Then he went over to the rolling cart and dragged it to the back of her car. He watched her a minute and noticed she kept rubbing the back of her head. He turned away and hunkered down to get to work. It took about twenty minutes to attach a new clamp that would hold the muffler in place. After checking to make sure it was secure, he slid out from under the car.

When he glanced at Little Mouse, he saw she was slumped down in the chair with her eyes closed. He approached her, making sure to step loudly, so she knew he was there. Her eyes jerked open, and she looked at him.

He smiled down at her. "Mufflers fixed. You okay."

"Yeah, just a bad headache," she said quietly. Then she rubbed the back of her head again.

He leaned towards her. "I know a trick. If you let me touch you, I can help," he beseeched her.

She stood and moved away, shaking her head no. As she moved back to her car, he noticed something in her hair at the back of her head. When he stepped closer, he easily saw the dried blood in the back of her blond hair.

"Jesus Little Mouse, you've got a cut on the back of your head," he said while reaching for her. Then he carefully tried to move her hair out of the way so he could get a better look. Just like before, she tried to wiggle away, and just like before he held tight. He found a huge knot there, with the blood dried in the middle.

He let go of her and clenched his fists. She was hurt bad, no wonder she had a headache. Making a quick decision, he told her "there's a doctor inside, and I need him to look at that."

She looked terrified and ready to bolt. "I had too much to drink the other night and fell," she lied. Instead of calling her out, he nodded and offered her his hand.

"Trust me Little Mouse," he pleaded.

"Cassie," she whispered. Then she slowly placed her tiny hand in his massive one.

Chapter Six
Cassie

Cassie stared at his big hand wrapped around hers. His palm was rough from hard work, and nothing like Parkers smooth one. Tingles spread through her body, just from that small touch. She missed holding hands. Parker had stopped right after they married, and now she didn't want to hold his hand. This biker however, she wished she could hold on to forever. There was something comforting in his touch.

Cassie wondered what it would be like to belong to this biker. He seemed rough on the outside, but would he be caring and sweet to someone he loved? She bet he would protect what was his with whatever means necessary. She bet he would consume the person he loved.

The biker stopped walking and squatted down to look into her eyes. "You okay Little Mouse? I seem to be loosing you", he asked.

All she could do was stare into his eyes. They were an amazing shade of the darkest blue she had ever seen. She bet at night they would look black.

"You keep staring at me like that, things are going to go a different way," he growled. "With you being married, I don't think that's a place we can take this."

Cassie could feel her face draining of colour. Parker had slammed her head off the wall for just looking at the biker. What would he do if he found out she had held his hand? Panicking now, she tried to pull her hand away.

"I changed my mind," she whispered. "I need to leave now." She tried backing up towards her car, desperate to get away.

The biker shook his head, and the next thing she knew she was up on his arms. She squeaked and held on. He powered across the parking lot and juggled her closer as he opened a door. Then they were inside the clubhouse.

Bikers turned in their direction, and she heard "here we go again," muttered from somewhere in the room.

"Steele," someone uttered. "What's up brother."

The biker turned to someone and asked where doc was. Then he told the man to get him, and off they went again. When she peeked her head up, she saw they were walking down a hall, and then they headed into a room.

He sat her gently on the edge of the bed, then moved to sit beside her. "There a reason why you keep trying to run Little Mouse," he questioned.

"I don't think my husband would like me being anywhere near you," she told him honestly.

"And what do you think he'd do if he found you with me?" He asked, then crossed his arms waiting for an answer.

She stared at him a minute, then muttered, "is your name really Steele?"

His brows drew together in frustration, but he answered her. "Steele's my road name, everyone has one. You met my brothers Navaho, Dagger and Trike by your car. Usually road names are given when you start with the club," he explained.

"What's your real name," she asked hesitatingly.

"Names Ryker," he told her. "But nobody uses it,"

She looked up at him, watching him watch her. "Can I use it," she whispered. "I don't really want to call you Steele."

He looked at her in shock for a minute. "No one has ever asked me what my given name was before. Everyone calls me Steele."

"Ryker," she reverently said. "I like that."

"I like the way it sounds on your lips," he told her softly. They stared at each other for a minute before she had to look away.

She made a decision, once the doc had checked out her head, she would go. Parker would kill her if he found her with Ryker, and she knew he would never give her up. He said as much the other night. There was no use loosing her heart to a man she could never have.

It was perfect timing when the doctor walked in.

Chapter Seven
Steele

Steele watched Cassie closely as the doctor entered the room. She seemed nervous and really unsure. He knew the doc could tell, and he smiled, instantly trying to put her at ease. Doc was really good with Ali, so he knew Cassie would be fine.

"I heard you might need me darling," he softly said. "What seems to be the problem?"

Steele watched as her back went straight and she sucked in breathe. A lone tear trailed down her cheek. "Please don't call me darling," she whispered. Then she was up and off the bed, "I'm fine, I'm just going to go."

Steele immediately stood up and blocked the door. She jolted slightly and backed up, looking between him and the doctor. She looked frightened now, and he hated it, all because the Doc had called her a name.

He raised his hands in a placating manner and went to speak, but Doc beat him to it. "What's your name?"

Cassie quietly told him her name. He smiled and told her she had a pretty name. "Steele asked me to take a look at you. If Steele is worried about something, you need to let me take a look. If you don't that boy will make my life hell for a long time. I'm not below begging," he teased.

Steele watched, mesmerized as a small smile tugged at her lips, then she nodded. The doc actually appeared relieved as he made his way closer to her. Cassie sat back down on his bed and faced the wall, sitting Indian style. Her back was to them and Steele could easily see the dried blood spot against her pretty blonde hair.

Doc looked to him and he shook his head, indicting they could talk later. Doc narrowed his eyes, but then headed over to Cassie.

"Can you just look down at your lap so I can get a good look? I'm going to need to touch you for a minute as I move your hair out of the way."

She nodded, then looked down. Steele moved back to the bed and sat down beside her. He watched as she slowly reached over and placed her hand in his. He curled his fingers around her small ones and scooted just a little closer.

He watched as she closed her eyes and pressed her lips together as Doc started to touch the area. He didn't like seeing her in pain. He was growing too close to her too quickly, but he didn't know if he could stop himself. He needed to do a little digging into her husband and see what was really going on.

Doc finally moved away and asked her to turn back around. When she did and was comfortable, he told her what he wanted to do.

"It's a bad lump you have there, and the cut should have had stitches. With it being two days old, it's unfortunately healing apart. If you let me, I can put three stitches in it and pull it back together. I'm really concerned about infection right now," he stated.

"I don't know," she said. "Would you be able to see them," she questioned.

"I have invisible thread, and they'll disintegrate, so nothing else would need to be done. But a head wound is tricky, you really need to let me help you. I can give you a quick shot near the wound and then you won't feel a thing," he explained. "I can also give you a prescription for the pain later. The stitches should make it a bit tender."

Doc looked to Steele and nodded. Steele then turned to Cassie and asked, "do you trust me Little Mouse?"

She looked at him a minute, then nodded. His heart swelled with pride. She had literally only seen him once before today and she trusted him!

He got her to turn back around on the bed, so her back was to the Doc once more. Next, he climbed on the bed and faced her. He moved as close as he could and lifted her legs over his. Then he carefully put his hand on the back of her neck and brought her head down, so her forehead rested on his chest. While he was doing that, Doc pulled his supplies out.

"Hold on to me Little Mouse," he demanded. Instantly, her small hands grabbed onto his biceps and held on. When doc gave her the needle she cried out. Steele held her neck tighter and tried his best to soothe her.

This was going to get complicated, Steele thought.

Chapter Eight
Cassie

The stitches were done, and the doctor had left. Ryker had assured her that he couldn't see them. The needle had hurt, but the stitches hadn't, although the doctor warned her that in an hour the numbing agent would wear off. He left her with a prescription for painkillers and another for antibiotics. He also told her to get in touch with him through Ryker if she had a need for him again.

Ryker was currently in the process of trying to talk her out of leaving. She was trying to ignore him as she walked down the hall.

"At least rest a bit before you leave Little Mouse," he pleaded. "You're gonna hurt bad in a little bit." She tried to tell him she'd be fine as she entered the common room. The bikers glanced her way, but she looked to floor and headed out the door.

"You can't drive," he protested when she reached her car.

"Ryker," she implored him. "I can't stay. I've been gone too long, I need to get home. I appreciate everything you and your club have done for me, but I can't be here any longer." She looked at him, begging him silently to understand.

"What are you afraid of?" He growled at her. "I know you're married, and I know he grabbed you at the restaurant. Is he always like that Little Mouse? Does he hurt you? There's something between us, and it draws me to you. I can help you."

She looked up at him. He felt the pull too. She felt safe with him, and she really wanted to stay. She wondered how different her life could be with him.

"Talk to me," he begged.

She leaned against her car and sighed. "I married three years ago, and I'm twenty three. Parker was sweet to me, and I've never had that. My parents never wanted me, and now they just want the connections I bring to the family. I cared for Parker, and when he showed me affection, I fell for him."

She looked up at Ryker. "I don't love him and don't think I ever have. He's been stressed lately is all, I'm sure he didn't mean to grab me." She wasn't going to tell him everything, just the quick version.

"I didn't have any reason to leave before, but I know now I can't stay with him anymore. I'll start getting things organized tomorrow and make it known to him and my parents that I'm done."

She looked up at him tentatively and waited. He stared at her intently.

"You end things, you come straight to me. You need anything, you come straight to me.

He hurts you, you come straight to me. I'm letting you know right now that you belong to me, and I protect what belongs to me. You say you've never known love, well be warned Little Mouse, I love with absolutely everything I have."

She stood there stunned. "I've met you twice," she whispered. The handsome man just smirked at her. Then, he leaned down and gave her the softest, lightest, most amazing kiss on the lips. When he pulled back, she realized at some point she had closed her eyes. She blinked them a couple times, then moved to open her door.

"Oh no," he said as he blocked her door. Then he motioned to a biker not to far away. The biker came over, and Ryker told him, "I'm driving Cassie home in her car, follow me and bring me back." The biker nodded and headed for a truck parked by the garage.

"You can't drive me home," she said panicking.

"No, but I can drive you to your street, then you only have to drive down the block." He stared at her, daring her to say no.

She smiled and agreed. If he was this protective, and they weren't together yet, she could only imagine what was coming.

She couldn't wait, she thought.

Chapter Nine
Cassie

Cassie sat in the driveway in her car. True to his word, Ryker had driven her to the corner then got out. She had gotten out too and rounded the car getting in the drivers seat. Her head was starting to hurt, but she didn't tell him.

He had crouched down in the doorway, so she sat with her legs dangling out. He took her phone and placed his number in it. He then told her that he put it under the name Rylie. She smiled at that, he was thinking of her safety again.

"Will you be okay," he asked seriously.

"I'll speak to my parents tonight and explain some things to them. When I get done with that, I'll make an appointment with my attorney. I won't tell my husband until I have to. I'll be okay," she told him.

He nodded, then kissed her on the forehead and let her go. She watched as he walked back to the truck. It was apparently Dagger that was driving it. After he climbed in, he took one last long look at her and he was gone.

Taking a deep breath, she spun around, so she was in the drivers seat and shut the door. On the way, Ryker had made her stop so he could fill her prescriptions. When he was back in the car, he had a bottle of water, and he watched as she washed down a couple pills. He was being so nice to her. She decided to keep most of what was happening to herself. She wanted to fix this without getting him involved. She wanted to protect him, just like he was protecting her.

She couldn't sit in the driveway forever, so she shut off the car, grabbed her purse and headed inside. Parker was in the dining room and there was paperwork spread out all over the table. He looked up when she entered.

"Where were you?" He didn't seem overly mad, so she told him.

"I went for a drive outside town. I saw some horses and stopped for awhile to pet them. I lost track of time, then my head started to hurt. So, I got back in the car and closed my eyes for a minute. I woke up a couple hours later. I didn't realize how tired I was. If you don't mind, I'm just going to go take a nap. I need to just sleep off this headache."

He stared at her a minute, then waved her off. She was surprised, but thankful and hurried to her room. Her head did hurt, but Ryker had assured her the painkillers would kick in soon.

She climbed onto her bed and pulled an afghan over herself. Then within minutes she was asleep.

When she woke, she was surprised to see it was five o'clock. Parker would want dinner. When she sat up, she realized her head wasn't too bad, so she freshened up in the bathroom, then headed to the kitchen. She took out the chicken breasts that she had marinating in the fridge and placed them on the griddle she kept near the stove. While they cooked, she steamed some vegetables and made a salad.

Parker and her ate in silence. When he was done, he told her he was heading back to the office and was gone. She cleaned up the dishes and tidied the house a bit. She knew she had plenty of time, because with Parker leaving the house after dinner, it meant he was going to see one of his girlfriends.

Her parents were very formal and expected her to call before showing up, so she took a minute to do that. When she told them she had some news, they seemed over joyed and told her to come right over. She didn't understand why they were so happy because she hadn't explained what the news was.

Two hours later, she walked back into her house in tears. Things with her parents hadn't gone so well.

Chapter Ten
Cassie

When Cassie got home, she was relieved to see Parker was still out. Her parents liked her to dress prim and proper, so the first thing she did was change into yoga pants and an off the shoulder sweatshirt. She figured Parker wouldn't like it, as he had many of the same beliefs as her parents, but he wasn't there.

She decided tonight was a wine night, so she poured herself a glass and turned on the fireplace in the sunken living room. Then she curled up in her favourite lounge chair and grabbed a book.

After fifteen minutes, she gave up. Thanks to her parents, she found she just couldn't concentrate. She closed it and tossed it onto the coffee table. Then, she leaned back and thought about what had happened tonight.

When she had pulled up to their house, both her parents had been waiting on the front step. She exited the car and made her way to them. Cassie's mother leaned forward and kissed her cheek, while her dad just held open the door for her.

Once they were sitting in the lounge with drinks, her mother asked what they news was. Cassie had taken a deep breath and told them she was making plans to leave Parker and to start divorce proceedings.

Her dad had sat there stoic while her mother had raised hell. Apparently, Parker was a perfect match for the family. He was from money and her father was grooming him to take over his law practice. Cassie had the perfect life her mother said, and she didn't want her to throw it away.

Cassie broke down then and had to tell them about some of the abuse. Her father then told her that Parker was just trying to get her in line. She needed to listen to him and try to be a better wife. She had been stunned, her father had actually agreed with Parker's actions.

Tears had fallen down her cheeks as she told them she couldn't do it anymore. She didn't love him, she was tired of the physical abuse and she hated that he slept with other woman.

Her mother had pretty much ordered her to stay with Parker. She told Cassie that when she phoned, they thought she was coming over to tell them she was pregnant. They basically demanded she go back and start on the grandchildren.

In tears, she had given up and walked out, still listening to them yelling at her as she shut her car door. Weren't parents supposed to be loving and supportive? She honestly had no idea what that would feel like.

On her way home, she had pulled over to the side of the road and pulled out her phone. She placed a call to her lawyer, knowing she would only be able to leave a message at this hour. Still, she wanted to start things moving.

When the front door opened, she was pulled from her thoughts. Parker walked in, closing the door behind him. When he spotted her in the living room, he headed her way. She nervously watched him approach. He stopped when he stood right in front of her.

"What are you dressed like that for?" He asked, looking down at her clothes in disgust. "What if I walked in the door with clients, you would have disgraced me!"

She just looked at him. He had never, not even once, brought clients home before. She had no idea where this was coming from. As he leaned in closer, she smelled the alcohol on his breath. That made her nervous. He hated drinking because it meant you weren't in total control of your actions. Something, had made him drink tonight, and a Parker with a few drinks in him, was a dangerous Parker.

He grabbed her by the arms and pulled her from the chair. While shaking her, he yelled right in her face.

"You dressed like this for that biker?" She didn't say a word, not sure if he knew she saw Ryker today. Her threw her to the floor before she could even form an answer and kicked her in the side. She screamed in pain as he turned and marched away.

It took her two hours to get off the floor and head to bed.

Chapter Eleven
Steele

Steele stood in the garage at the clubhouse. He was leaning against a tool bench and he had a beer in his hand. Preacher was tweaking his hog while he watched. It had been two days since he had seen Little Mouse and he was getting angsty. He needed to talk to her, and he needed to know if she was okay.

He had shot her off a couple quick texts, but they were vague, as he pretended to be Rylie. He had one of his brothers digging into Parker's background, but so far all he found was the man grew up with a fucking silver spoon in his mouth.

Steele wasn't sure how to feel about Cassie's life. She had obviously grown up well off, and she was used to high end living. Steele had some dough in the bank, but nothing like she was accustomed to. He had his hog, and he had his room at the clubhouse. Maybe it was time to talk to Preacher about starting on his cabin, out back, near Jaxon and Ali's.

He was so caught up in his thoughts, he didn't realize Preacher had grabbed a beer and was studying him.

"What's stuck in your head brother," he questioned. Steele sighed and turned to his prez.

"Cassie," he growled. "I swear to christ, that fuck of a husband hurts her. She had bruising on her arms and I saw a faint bruise on her cheek. Not to fucking mention the head wound, and it was bad. She didn't outright say it was her husband, but she didn't deny it either. I'm not sure what else I can do, shy of killing the fucker." Steele balled his hands into fists, liking that idea more and more.

"First off," Preacher said, "she needs to admit her man is beating her. And two, if her husband's a pillar of society, people will notice if he goes missing. Let's do some more digging and figure this shit out. You said she's started taking steps to leave him, so let's help her with that. Maybe we should have church and see what the brothers can come up with."

Just as Steele was about to respond, Preachers phone went off. Preacher grabbed it and listened for a second. As whatever brother it was kept talking, Preacher's expression got darker and darker. Then he hung up and was on the move.

"Five cop cars pulling up to the gate. I have no idea what the hell is going on. Gather the brothers, and make sure if they're carrying it's a registered piece, if not get it locked up. We got maybe five minutes before the shit hits the fan. I'll do some stalling at the gate."

Steele and Preacher then broke off. Preacher headed for the front gate while Steele headed into the clubhouse. It took him seconds to get things locked down, they didn't need to give the cops a reason to lock up any brothers.

Literally, a minute later, about ten cops, both in uniform and in suits flooded the clubhouse. The cops weren't messing around and had their pieces drawn. Shouts were echoing off the walls, demanding that all the brothers lay on their stomachs on the floor.

Preacher refused this, saying the brothers would kneel, but no way in hell would they lay on the floor. The brothers didn't wait for the cops to answer, they knew how this would go, so they all got to their knees and waited. After every brother was searched for weapons, and the cops came up dry, things seemed to go a little easier.

Then one of the suits came over to Steele. "We got tipped this club was trafficking illegal weapons, and you were the man behind it. We need to search this compound, but particularly your room and bike."

Two agonizing hours later, the cops left. They of course, found nothing. The clubhouse and garage were a mess that was an easy fix. Steele's room and hog were a different story. Some pieces of his hog were still laying on the ground, but Navaho already headed in that direction, stating it would be fucking fixed.

Steele's room was another story. His bedding was slashed, his dresser had been dumped, all his product, including shampoo, liquid soap, and whatever else they could find was dumped on his bathroom floor. His room was fucking trashed, and Steele and the rest of the brothers were furious.

Preacher looked at Steele as he roared with unleashed violence. The only person with a grudge and connections was fucking Parker.

Chapter Twelve
Cassie

It had been two days since Parker had come home drunk and kicked her. Cassie was still hurting. She was pretty sure she had either a bruised rib or a cracked rib, but she didn't think it was broken. Thankfully, her husband had left her alone since then. He was still mean, but he hadn't touched her.

It was early in the morning so Cassie grabbed a quick shower then decided to start breakfast. She only had to deal with Parker for about a half hour before he left for work. She started the bacon, then cracked the eggs into a pan for his fried egg. Once everything was close to being done, she put down his toast.

She was just placing his meal on the table when he came downstairs. He didn't look at her as he dug into his food. He had a folder open that he was reading through as he ate. When it looked like he was done, she took his plate into the kitchen and rinsed it off.

When she heard him call for her, she went back to him. Without any emotion he told her to sit. Then he just studied her for a minute, she hated when he did that. It always unnerved her.

"Yesterday evening, I had your boyfriends clubhouse raided. This morning I will receive a call, letting me know how many bikers are in jail. They hit the whole club, but their main focus was Steele." He stopped and watched her again. "You can deny it all you want, that you two aren't dating, but I saw the way you eyed him in the restaurant, and I'm not an idiot. You married me, you belong to me," he roared.

She cringed as she realized what he had done. Ryker and his friends could be in jail, and it was all her fault. He had met her only a couple times, and she was ruining his life.

He stood up then and waved the file in front of her face. "I have information on every member of that biker gang, and I plan on using it. You will not see him again." He tilted his head and looked at her. "Get you phone," he demanded.

She didn't move fast enough, so he slammed both his hands on the table. When he took a step towards her, she scrambled to do as he wanted. So ran to her room, grabbed her purse and pulled out her phone, then she went back him. As she walked back in the room, his phone rang. He answered, listened for a minute, then slammed it on the table. He told her no arrests were made. His face was red with anger.

He snatched up her phone and demanded. "Call him and tell him you love me and you're done with him. Tell him he's just a biker and you want a real man."

When a tear slid down her face, he smacked her and she fell against the table. Instantly, her side started to hurt again. "Call him," he screamed as he shoved the phone into her hands.

Trembling, she hit Ryker's number. As the phone rang, more tears streamed down her face.

She heard him pick up, and then his voice came over. "Little Mouse," he said urgently. "You okay?"

"Yes," she whispered.

"I need to see that for myself Cassie. Can you meet me?"

She closed her eyes so she couldn't see her husband hovering over her. "I can't see you anymore. I love my husband and I need to stay with him," she told him quietly.

"He's there with you right now, isn't he?" He waited a minute and when she finally said yes he continued. "You still want to leave him and figure things out with me," he asked. Again she whispered yes to him.

"You hang in there Little Mouse, I'm coming for you. I'm on a run, but I can be there in just over an hour. I told you I'd protect you, and I will. I know you don't know me that well, but you need to trust me. I'm falling hard for you, and I'm not going to lose you. My club brother believes in soul mates, and you're mine. I'm on my way Cassie."

Then the phone went dead, and she stared at it, sobbing now. She turned to her husband and told him, "he hung up on me."

Her husband just smiled, and it gave her the shivers.

Chapter Thirteen
Cassie

Cassie watched Parker hesitantly, something had changed. His smile was almost evil, and it creeped her out. He was usually emotionless, not really caring about her, and basically leaving her alone. As long as she acted like a dedicated wife, he went about his way. Today though, she seemed to be the focus of his attention. It's almost like he was jealous and trying to stake his claim.

"I got a call last night." He moved closer to her as he spoke. "Your parents told me it's time we gave them some grandbabies, and I think I agree." He reached out quickly and latched on to her arm painfully. She twisted and kicked as he dragged her to the living room. Her size hampered her, and she could do nothing as he hurled her to the carpeted floor. She threw out her arm to try to break her fall, but she landed funny.

She screamed in pain as her wrist snapped. She had never felt that much agony before. She tried to roll away, but he was suddenly there, covering her body with his and pinning her to the ground. She felt him push her dress up, and then he ripped it down the front. She could do nothing but sob as he raped her.

When he left the room and headed to the bathroom, she pulled her dress together and sat up. She hurt and just wanted Ryker, but he was still too far away. She knew her wrist was broken, and she cradled it close to her body.

She stood and slowly made her way into the garage. Looking around, she quickly located what she was looking for. Parker kept a bag with his old baseball supplies on a shelf in the corner. With one hand it was difficult, but she managed to drag it down. She got it open and pulled out the baseball bat. It felt good in her hands.

Quietly, she made her way back into the living room and headed towards the bathroom. She passed it so she was standing on the opposite side. This way, when he came out, he would head back towards the living room and hopefully not even notice her.

It was an agonizing wait. Her wrist throbbed, and it was hard to get a good grip on the bat. She had to hold it in her left hand and use her right arm for support. It was awkward, but she hoped it would give her enough reinforcement to swing the bat hard enough to do some damage.

Finally, the water stopped running, and she heard the door start to open. She spread her legs a bit and got ready. He came out of the bathroom and headed towards the living room, not even looking in her direction as she had hoped. She swung the bat as hard as she could and it connected with the side of his head.

Parker fell, grabbing the spot on his head and moaning. She moved forward, raised the bat and this time she got him just below his right knee. He screamed, letting go of his head to grab his leg. He tried to get up, but his leg didn't hold him and he fell back down. He turned to face her and the look of fury on his face had her backing up.

She turned, keeping a hold on the bat and ran for the door. He was getting up again and trying to follow. She didn't even stop to put on shoes, she threw the door open and hurried out. She held on to the bat with one hand, and her dress together with the other. She headed for the back of the property and ran straight into the trees.

She figured it would take a good two hours to reach the compound on foot, and it would be painful without shoes, but she could do it. She didn't want to see Ryker, she just wanted the comfort of being near him until she could figure out what to do. She didn't want to bring anymore trouble to his club. Crying and in a lot of pain, she headed out. She remembered Ryker's sweet kiss as she walked and held tight to that memory.

Chapter Fourteen
Steele

Steele revved the throttle and forced the bike faster down the highway, with Cassie on the brain. Her phone call had rattled him. He knew she wasn't breaking up with him. Her husband was in the background and forcing her to make that call. Steele had heard the tears in her voice and something in him broke. He really cared about his Little Mouse and he really didn't want her hurt.

When he got near the exit he slowed, not wanting to roll the bike. His brothers stuck with him, taking the same turn off. He slowed on the side streets and made his way to her street. Once near her house he began to feel agitated. He had no idea what he was about to walk into, his Little Mouse had been afraid on the phone.

All the bikes roared into her long driveway and parked near the house. Pieces were drawn as they made their way to the front door in a group. Dagger had military training, so he took lead. Steele wanted to just kick the door in and raise hell, but Dagger held him back and told to be smart. The club already considered her his, so they would do whatever he needed.

The door had been left unlocked, so slowly Dagger pushed it open and made his way inside. Steele stuck close to his back and his brothers followed. The house was quiet, eerily quiet. Dagger headed into the main part of the house and motioned for some of the brothers to head upstairs. It was surprising how silent a group of bikers wearing shit kickers could be.

The dining room and kitchen were clear, so they headed to the living room. Something's had been knocked over and it looked like there had been a bit of a fight. Other than that, it was clear.

Trike came downstairs with the rest of the club and stated all was clear upstairs. Dagger headed off to check the garage, and some of the boys went to take a closer look around. Navaho moved into the living room and started looking around.

Dagger returned. Apparently, Cassie's car was still there, but the other spot was empty. It was odd, with the front door being unlocked. Would they leave and not lock it? Trike came back holding a purse. Dagger left and came back into the room holding Cassie's cell phone.

Dread was starting to make its way up Steele's chest. No woman left the house without a cell or a purse. It just wasn't done. He looked up as Navaho motioned him over. His brothers eyes were troubled.

He pointed to a small spot on the carpet. "Blood with some semen mixed in it brother," he stated. "My bet, unless your girl was a virgin, she was forced." Navaho stood then and locked his hand on his shoulder. "I'm sorry brother," he said quietly. "Club is family, we'll move together and find her, then we take him out."

"Move out," Preacher ordered, and the brothers left the house. Steele took his Little Mouse's purse and phone with him. Once outside, Preacher told the brothers to drive around and see if they could find Parker's black BMV convertible. They only had a short window until it would be too dark to see.

All the brothers mounted their hogs and started them up. They left the driveway in two's, each group heading in a different direction. The brothers were furious, and they were all hoping to be the one to find Parker. Steele just hoped they didn't do too much damage to the fucker if they found him. Steele needed to get his shot too.

Preacher held Steele back when he went to take off as well. "Hold up brother," he said. "I want you at the clubhouse with me. If she comes looking for you, you need to be there. We don't know what shape she's gonna be in."

Steele nodded his understanding and then roared down the driveway and turned in the direction of the clubhouse. He needed his Little Mouse in his arms, and he wouldn't rest until that happened.

Chapter Fifteen
Cassie

Cassie stumbled and fell again. She thought that was the fourth time, but she wasn't sure. Her feet were bleeding badly, and they hurt, each step sending fire up her legs. She had no idea how long she'd been walking, but the sun was low in the sky, so she knew darkness wasn't far away. Without a watch or her phone, there was no way to check the time.

She had tried to tie the top of her dress together, but with one hand it didn't go so well. She got it so her chest was covered, but the top of her bra was visible. The woods were empty though, so she didn't have to worry about someone seeing her.

She had ripped a bit off the bottom of her dress, so it now hung to mid-thigh. It was short, but it still covered her. She used the strip to make a makeshift sling. It now cradled her broken wrist to her chest and seemed to help a bit. She still had to be careful though, as the slightest touch brought her to her knees. She had fallen on it once, and it caused her to see black spots. She had thrown up when her stomach rolled, then picked herself back up and kept walking.

After that, if she tripped, she made sure to roll a bit and land on her side. She was hungry, but she had nothing to eat or drink. She didn't think her poor stomach could hold anything, anyway.

She was certain she was headed in the right direction. As a kid, she used to play in these woods with her friends. She used to love playing hide and seek, so she wasn't afraid to be in them all alone. She actually found the woods peaceful. She loved how quiet and peaceful they were

She thought back to Parker. Since her marriage to him, he had always been cruel, but only verbally, not physically. Even after her wedding night, they had only slept together a few times. After that, he slept with other girls and left her alone. He hadn't even kissed her, unless they were out in public and then he did it for show.

The rape had hurt her deeply, both physically and mentally. He had hit her a couple times in the last few months, but nothing was as bad as the last couple days. She had suffered a head wound, possibly a cracked rib and now the rape. She was scared now, as she didn't want him to find her. In fact, she just wanted to hide from everyone for a bit.

Her lawyer had called and told her that he couldn't help her, he knew Parker too well and it would be a conflict of interest. After six more phone calls and receiving the same response, she figured it was going to be difficult to get out of this marriage. It was obvious Parker had anticipated what she would do and had taken actions to stop her. She was running out of options.

She also knew he was probably looking for her. She had got him pretty good with the baseball bat. He had been furious when she left, and the thought of what he would do to her terrified her. She knew she couldn't go back to the house, but with no money, cell or clothes her options were limited.

She knew Ryker would help her, but she didn't want to bring trouble to his club. She was sure that would be the first place Parker would look for her.

It was starting to get dark now, so she slowed her pace and used the bat as a crutch. She was surprised when she came across the lake at the back of the clubs property. She hadn't realized she was that close.

Looking around, she found a pine tree that had branches touching the ground. She crawled underneath and ignored the scratches on her skin from the needles. It was soft and warmer under here, so she curled herself up into a ball and tried to sleep. Ryker was close, so she could relax now.

Chapter Sixteen
Steele

Steele was loosing his mind. It was midmorning and his Little Mouse had been gone all night. She was hurting and there was nothing he could do. He had even gone out on his own last night, desperate to do anything but sit on his ass and wait.

Dagger and Trike entered the clubhouse and Steele headed their way. They looked tired, but they shook their heads at silent question.

Dagger spoke up, "Parker's car was seen all over town last night, but Cassie wasn't with him. Folks I questioned said he appeared to be looking for something. Also heard he had a cut on the side of his head and was limping. Looks like your girl fought back," Dagger said proudly.

"Still, she's out there somewhere and she's hurt. I need to find her," Steele said brokenly.

He stomped to the bar, grabbed a bottle of whiskey and poured up a shot. He slammed it back and enjoyed the burn it caused. He poured another, and shot it back as well, then threw the glass at the wall. It shattered into a million tiny pieces and Steele felt it in his heart.

Steele's cell went off in his pocket. He pulled it out and looked at the screen. It was the prospect manning the gate. He told him the cops were here again, and since they had a search warrant, he had to let them in. Two cars were pulling up to the clubhouse now.

Steele roared his frustration and then relayed the message to his brothers. Preacher headed to the doors and opened them, as the cops stepped in, followed by Parker. Steele stood his ground with his fists clenched tight.

"We have a warrant," one of the cops stated. "One, Cassandra Holt, has been reported missing, and we have reason to believe she may have been abducted by this motorcycle gang. We expect you to cooperate while we search the premises."

Preacher moved out of the way and spread his arms out in welcome. "Have at it boys," he told them with a smirk. Then he made his way to Steele.

"Calm brother," he told him loud enough for everyone to hear. "She's not here, so there's nothing to worry about. This prick just wants to rile you up. He knows she's done with his sorry ass and he's desperate."

Steele smirked, while Parker looked like he was going to blow a gasket. Steele went back to the bar and took a seat, while two cops flanked Parker, talking to him harshly.

An hour later the cops returned, without his Little Mouse. They spoke to Preacher quietly, then left. Parker glared at Steele and he could only laugh at the fury on his face, then he too was gone.

"Well that was fun," Dagger stated sarcastically. "I guess we should have a look and see how much damage was done this time." The brothers all sighed and headed to their rooms.

Steele's was still pretty fucked up from before, but nothing new had been done to it. He made his way to the garage. Cabinets and tool chests had been moved, but thankfully nothing was damaged. He muscled everything back into place, then headed back into the clubhouse.

His spirits were pretty low, and he didn't know where to turn. Preacher walked up to him and clapped him on the back. "Things always work out brother. We'll find your girl and you'll get your chance." Preacher looked him square in the eye. "Maybe it's time for you to start your own cabin," he advised.

Another cell went off, and Steele and Preacher looked over to Navaho as he pulled his out and looked at the screen. "Dragon", Navaho told them, then put it up to his ear. He listened for a minute then shoved it back in his pocket.

"Dragon says Ali saw someone in the woods by their cabin. He checked it out, but came up empty. He wants me to come out and scout the area a bit. Might be nothing, might be something," he said. "Think maybe you should come with," he told Steele.

Steele dropped his head and prayed, then he pushed out the door behind his brother.

Chapter Seventeen
Cassie

Cassie huddled under the tree. The night had been colder than she expected, and even though the sun was shining, she was still shivering. She couldn't move, her body was weak, but she was covered in sweat. How could she be covered in sweat, but still be cold? She couldn't think straight, and all she could do was pull her knees up closer to body and try to warm herself up.

Branches snapped in the distance and she held perfectly still to listen. She heard it again, but this time closer. Someone was coming, and she prayed to god it wasn't Parker. Although, she knew Parker would never think to search the woods for her, and if he did, he would probably only end up getting lost in them.

The noise was getting closer, and now she could make out footsteps. They certainly weren't trying to be stealthy as they were heavy and seemed to be headed directly for her. She knew immediately it was Ryker. Only a huge biker could stomp through the woods like that.

She tried to wiggle her body closer to the low-hanging branches, but it wouldn't cooperate. She could only lay there and wait, crying softly as she realized there was no way she could escape now. His club was going to be involved and she couldn't stop it.

There was a loud snap, and she gasped as the branches were literally torn from the tree. Sunlight hit her face, making it hard to see. Then a huge body loomed over her and she sobbed as Ryker looked down at her.

"I was trying to protect you," she whispered. "Parker will come after you if you help me. I don't want you or your club hurt," she cried.

Ryker only shook his head. "Not your problem Little Mouse," he told her. "The fight is now ours, you're not to worry about that any more." Then he was climbing in the tree and reaching for her.

"My wrist is broken," she quickly told him. "My feet hurt from walking, but I'm okay." She signed as he placed his hand on her cheek.

"You're not okay," he told her. "But from here on out, you're never going to feel pain again. You're under my protection." He then carefully slipped one arm under her knees and the other under her back. With little effort he hefted her into the air and cradled her against his massive chest.

Cassie curled into his warmth as her her body continued to shake with the shivers. Navaho seemed to appear out of nowhere and he gently placed his hand on her forehead.

"Girls burning up," he told Ryker. "Doc's at Ali's, I'll head there and grab him," he growled. Cassie turned to thank him, but he was already gone, swallowed up by trees.

"He's like a ninja," Cassie whispered.

"Na, not a ninja Little Mouse, just an Indian who believes in the old ways." He cradled her closer and his footsteps moved faster. In no time he had reached the clubhouse, and he was juggling her as he grabbed the handle and threw open the door.

There was no noise as he stepped inside. Cassie lifted her head and looked around at the bikers.

Dagger stepped forward. "Your room's straightened and ready, Navaho called and told us you found your girl. Doc should be here in twenty. Soup is on in the kitchen, I'll dish up a bowl and bring it to you."

Ryker nodded and then moved away heading to his room. Cassie wondered just how messy Ryker was if the guys needed to straighten his room before she could see it.

Ryker kicked open the door, then froze as he stepped inside. Cassie lifted her head and laughed. There was a pretty flowery peach bedspread on his bed, with pretty peach pillows spread on top.

"Fucking bikers," she heard Ryker growl.

Chapter Eighteen
Steele

Steele was fuming as he started the shower for his Little Mouse. Her dress was practically falling off her, and she had tried to tie it back together. Her wrist was broken, her feet had been torn up slightly and she was running a fever. Not to mention, she had been raped. To think, her husband had done that too her. He really hoped his brothers found the fucker quickly. He'd definitely let Dragon get out his blowtorch and play.

Steele made sure the water was only slightly warm. He didn't want to make it too hot and cause her fever to spike, but he couldn't stand to see her shivering with the chills. Figuring it should be okay, he moved back into the bedroom. He pulled a pair of his sweats out of his dresser and grabbed a clean shirt. He moved back into the bathroom and laid them on the counter.

Walking back to the bed, he scooped her up and carried her into the bathroom. He set her on the side of the bathtub and squatted down in front of her. Slowly, he raised his hand and carefully undid her halfhearted knot. Holding the dress together with one hand, he took her good hand in his free one and moved it to the front of her dress. When she had a hold of it, he let go and smiled down at her. Even crouching on the floor, he was taller than her.

"I'm going to leave you alone now. Clothes are on the counter and there's a fresh towel on the rod. Please don't be too long because the water isn't very hot. I don't want your fever to get worse. If you need me, call out. I won't leave the bedroom." Then he kissed her lips softly and stood, leaving the room.

He laughed as she squealed, figuring she was under the spray now. Not ten minutes later the shower shut off. Five more minutes, and she was calling out for him. He made his way back in and shook his head at the sight.

His pants were miles too long and there was no way she could walk. She was desperately trying to hold them up, but she was having trouble as the shirt fell over it to her knees.

She smiled slightly and admitted, "I think I'm stuck."

"I think you are too," he agreed with a smirk. He moved close and once again squatted on the floor. He grabbed the sweats with one hand, then lifted the shirt with the other. He told her to hold the shirt up so he could see. He tied the drawstring, then rolled the waistband down about five times. Next, he rolled up each of the legs another five times.

"You're so fucking tiny," he told her. Then he once again scooped her up, carrying her into the bedroom. When he sat down, he placed her on her lap.

"I'm so fucking proud of you," he told her. "You fought back and actually hurt the ass. Then you got away and made your way on foot to me. And to top it all off, you're still trying to protect the club. When the time is right, and all this is over, I'm officially gonna make you mine."

She reached up and grabbed his shirt with her good hand, pulling him down closer. Then she kissed him. He loved it, but immediately deepened it. His tongue swept inside and he felt her tentatively touch it with her own. He grabbed the back of her head and dominated her mouth. When he pulled away, she was panting heavily.

Steele smirked, then placed her on the bed. He grabbed a brush and moved behind her. She sighed in obvious pleasure as he took his time brushing out the knots. He finished just as the doctor arrived.

Chapter Nineteen
Steele

Steele sat close to his Little Mouse as Doc stepped into the room. He was pleased to see she was smiling at the Doc, not at all nervous about being around him this time.

"I see you've had a bit of trouble sweetheart. Let's take a look at you, and I'll see what I can do to fix you up," Doc told her kindly.

The first thing he did was check out her broken wrist. She whimpered and buried her head in Steele's chest, as Doc prodded a bit at the swelled area.

"It looks like a perfect break. What I need you to do is ice it for about fifteen minutes at a time, every couple hours. I can put a splint on it for now, and that will keep your wrist nice and straight. Hopefully, in a couple days, the swelling will be down enough that I can put a cast on it for you," he explained. Then he got out his supplies, and in minutes she was in a splint and a sling. "Keep it elevated," he told her.

The Doc then moved down to her feet and looked them over pretty thoroughly. "You've got them pretty clean," he said happily. "I'll apply some ointment and wrap them for you. You should be able to walk on them, just use some caution. I want them cleaned each day though, and new ointment applied."

He then got to work there as Steele watched in concern. His girl held tightly to his arm, but didn't utter one word. He was so proud of her. Doc then applied a bit more ointment to some of her cuts and scratches and addressed her fever.

"Your fever isn't too bad sweetheart. I'll give you some painkillers for the wrist and some penicillin for the fever. That will also help with infection too. You will probably feel better with some food in your tummy and a lot of rest," he told her.

Steele thanked the Doc then and walked him out. Once the door was shut, he pulled out his cell and called Navaho. The Indian answered right away.

"Brother, you got any soup you can warm up for my girl," he asked.

"Hot and ready," Navaho answered. "Just waiting on your okay to bring it to you."

Steele chuckled. The Indian was always ahead of them all. "I need some ice too for her wrist."

"Will do. I'll crush it a bit first, so it moulds more to her wrist. Be there in five," he said, then promptly hung up.

Steele just shook his head and climbed back on the bed with his Little Mouse. The poor thing was exhausted, and almost asleep, but she looked up at him sadly, as he pulled her close.

He made sure to prop her wrist up on his chest.

"He raped me," she whispered brokenly, as tears formed to wet her cheeks. He didn't want to explain to her that they'd already figured that out.

"Aw, Little Mouse," he said. "Your husband isn't a man. A wife should be treasured and treated with the utmost care. It's what I plan to do with you, for the rest of your life. We'll get you a divorce and then you're mine. But no more protecting the club, that stops now. It's my job to protect you. That bastard won't get anywhere near you again, you can count on that."

"You still want me after that," she questioned quietly.

"Still want you," he laughed. "If you weren't so banged up, I'd show you how much I want you," he smirked. Then he got serious again. "I'm so sorry you had to go through that, and I'll do everything I can to make it better. I'm falling for you Little Mouse, and it's killing me to see you so hurt."

"I'm falling for you to Ryker," she told him with a smile.

"And there's the smile I love," he declared happily. "There's gonna be a lot more of those from now on," he promised her.

Chapter Twenty
Steele

Steele stared at the tiny woman tangled up in
his sheets. Her long blonde hair was spread
out on his pillow, and she looked like an angel.
He had no idea how someone could hurt her.
She had a huge heart and had so much love to
give, yet no one had shown her love back.

He kneeled on the bed and crawled over to
her. Her brushed some hair off her cheek and
then kissed it. Her skin was warm and soft. She
stirred slightly, but didn't wake up. He trailed
his mouth over to her lips and nibbled on
them. When her breath caught and her mouth
opened, he knew she had awakened. He
plunged his tongue inside and met hers.

They kissed for several minutes, and then he pulled back. "You taste good," he told her.

"I want to be woken like that all the time," she declared, as she blinked the sleep out of her eyes.

"The lady from the banks here. I've got her waiting at one of the tables by the bar. Church is typically only for men, so you being in there was pretty much a one-time thing. We can use Preacher's office though, if you want more privacy."

She shook her head. "The tables fine," she replied. "Just give me a minute in the bathroom and we can go out." Then she scooted around him and climbed off the bed, heading to the bathroom. Steele shook his head, even the bed was a bit high for her.

A few minutes later, she came out looking more awake. He looked at her clothes and told her, "maybe we should have borrowed some of Ali's clothes for you."

"Nope," she said forcefully. "If I'm going to wear someone else's clothes, I'd really rather they be yours. I like your clothes, they smell good," she declared. Then as if to prove her point, she lifted up the sleeve and sniffed it, smiling happily.

"You're a nut," he told her. Then he walked over and picked her up, heading out the door with her.

"You know," she started, "the doctor said I can walk."

"What did you say," he said. "I can't hear you." She just smiled and snuggled in closer.

About a third of the club ended up being in the main room when they entered, along with the girl from the bank. Cassie got a look at her, and then looked up at him.

"I understand everything now. Does the lawyer look like that too?"

Steele looked over to the banker. She had on a really short pencil skirt, her blouse was open pretty low. Her kitten heels and long, teased out dark hair finished the look. "The lawyers a man," he growled.

He sat Cassie at the table, then took a seat beside her. Preacher sat on the other side as her, and the banker sat across from her. Preacher introduced the woman and then they got down to business.

"What accounts are you aware of," the banker asked.

"We have a joint account that we use for house bills and everyday things. We have a high interest savings account that basically we just put money in and let it build up. We also have an RRSP each. I also have two separate accounts that hold two different inheritances. They are both solely in my name," she explained.

The banker looked at both Steele and Preacher before she turned back to Cassie. Steele leaned in closer, knowing this was going to be bad.

"Your joint account has a balance of a couple hundred dollars in it. Your joint savings has about a thousand. Both your RRSP's have been cleaned out and one of your inheritance accounts is empty. The other one is fine, and I've put a lock on that one. It seems like over the last day or two someone has been trying to access that one as well." The banker stopped then, waiting for his Little Mouse's reaction.

Chapter Twenty One
Cassie

Cassie stared at the woman speechless. Ryker grabbed her good hand and pulled it into his lap, then he pushed his chair up close to hers. She leaned into him, taking all the support he was silently offering. Parker had taken basically everything.

"Parker went to University," she started. "His parents paid for it. I worked full time to support us and took some college writing courses at night. Parker told me I didn't need a University education, he would make enough money to support us both. He liked the idea of me staying home. I worked my ass off as he finished University and went on to Law

School. He was immediately given a job at my fathers firm when he graduated."

She stopped then and looked at them all. "I don't care about any of that anymore. I was young, I still am, and I was stupid. I did what he asked without thought. He's been playing me since he met me. I don't care about the joint accounts, they don't matter to me. It's sad he took my RRSP, but it's not the end of the world." She looked directly to the banker then. How did he get access to my inheritance?"

The banker pulled a piece of paper from a folder and slid it across the table. It was the account her parents had set up for her and the paper had their signatures on it giving Parker access. They basically handed him everything.

"They also signed a piece of paper allowing him access to your other inheritance account. Your husband has also taken out a court order to try to get access to the account. Now, since the account was set up as part of a will, and since it was left solely to you, no one can really touch it. I do suggest you see a lawyer though. He can go to court for you and easily have the document thrown out. Unfortunately, there is pretty much a zero chance of seeing any of the other money again."

Cassie smiled at the other woman. "I don't care about any of it. My parents money has always come with a price tag. In a way, I'm glad to see that go. The other inheritance was left to me by my grandfather, and I loved him dearly. My parents resented me for getting that money and tried over the years to take it from me. I'll talk to the lawyer because my grandfather made it clear, that money was for me."

"Okay then," the woman stated. "I will take over the handling of that account personally. That being said, anyone that wants access to it, will have to come to me directly. I can guarantee, no one will get near it. If that's all, I'll be off. If you need anything, you can reach me through the club."

The woman then got up, kissed Preacher passionately on the lips, turned and winked at her, then left. Cassie giggled and told the boys, "I like it here." Laughter could be heard throughout the room.

Preacher turned to Cassie. "The lawyer will be here first thing in the morning. We'll get him to throw out that fucking inheritance paperwork. Doc should be here later tonight, and he said he'd have all the paperwork with him. We want everything documented good," he told her. "Is there anything you want from your house," he asked.

Cassie thought about it. "My birth certificate and passport are in the safe, but other than that nothing. I don't even want my clothes, they weren't me anyway. I would like my laptop though. I've been writing for years, and everything's saved on that computer, as well as an eternal hard drive that I keep stored with it."

"I'll send a couple brothers there this afternoon to get all that."

She teared up then. "Thank you, for everything," she told him.

Preacher walked over to the bar then and reached under it. He came back with a black

Harley t-shirt and handed it to her. "You belong with us now," he declared.

Chapter Twenty Two
Steele

The next two days went by in a blur. His Little
Mouse had come out of her shell. She
definitely seemed to enjoy being around his
brothers, and he couldn't be happier. The
brothers were all falling in love with her, and
Trike had even invaded their room and put up
stars, just as he had for Ali. And, just like Ali,
Cassie had kissed his cheek when she saw
them. Now Steele understood how Dragon
felt, and he agreed with him, Trike was
fucking fast.

Doc had come by with all the paperwork he
had as evidence of Parker's abuse. The lawyer
had also come by and got the paperwork

started for the divorce. He also filed a motion to have the inheritance paperwork thrown out, which of course was a success. And, he went to the police station and started the paperwork for a restraining order.

The detective friend of the lawyers was helpful, but he advised them that Cassie really needed to head down to the station and show herself. That would get all the crooked cops that Parker had in his pocket, to back off.

The only problem that was left, was how to serve Parker. He had disappeared after that first day of sightings. The lawyer had assured them though, that even if he didn't get served, it was all on record, and that was the important part.

The boys had gone to the house and gotten the paperwork and the laptop that Cassie wanted. The house was quiet, and it didn't even look like Parker had been there. The boys hadn't taken any clothes, but they brought her everything they could find in her bathroom. This meant that she now smelled like peaches, instead of smelling like him.

Steele had also gotten Dragon to bring Ali over. The two had spent hours together holed up in his room. He figured they both could use a friend, and since Ali had gone through something similar to Cassie's situation, he hoped Ali could help her. They had come out with tears drying on their cheeks and huge smiles on their faces. Both himself and Dragon had been fucking thrilled.

That afternoon, Ali had left and come back with eight bags from Walmart. Steele had loaded her up with cash and told her to pick some shit out. The girls were almost identical in body shape and size, so he figured it would be easy for her.

Cassie had gushed over the cheap jeans, yoga pants, shirts, underwear and shoes. Then, Steele had presented her with another bag, this one he had bought after Ali told him her size.

Cassie had cried when she pulled out the black riding boots, helmet and soft black leather jacket. The paperwork was filed, so as far as Steele was concerned she was now a free agent, and he was staking his claim.

That night they had a BBQ. Navaho cooked and Trike got the booze. Then they lit a huge fire and roasted marshmallows. Steele loved watching the happiness pour out of his Little Mouse. She really didn't care about the money he realized. That was good because Steele had started work on his own cabin. It was down from Dragons, and far enough away that the trees obscured their view of each other.

All the brothers laughed and drank, but not enough to get drunk. Everyone of them remembered what happened the last time they had a BBQ, and nobody wanted a repeat.

Guards were posted and everyone had their piece hidden on them. Cassie had no idea of the slight tension amongst them, the brothers made sure of that. The next morning they were headed to the police station to meet with the detective, and Steele had no idea how that would turn out.

Chapter Twenty Three
Cassie

Today, Cassie was headed to the police station. She was extremely nervous, but at the same time, she couldn't wait to get this over with. She loved the club and didn't want any more trouble to come their way because of her. She needed Parker stopped, and she needed him found.

She dressed in a new pair of black jeans, she wore a blue t-shirt, and she finally had on her new motorcycle jacket and boots. Ryker had wanted to take a cage, but she insisted on going on the bike. She had never ridden before and was really excited about getting the chance.

Ryker took her hand and towed her towards his bike. He stopped beside it and reached out to grab her helmet off the seat. When he turned to put it on her head, he stopped and chuckled. She was so excited she was bouncing on her feet. When he shook his head and glanced at his brothers, they were laughing as well. His Little Mouse was cute!

When she asked why she was the only one wearing a helmet, he explained state laws deemed you didn't have to wear one. She scowled at that, so he tweaked her nose, then climbed on. He held out his hand, and she awkwardly climbed on behind him.

He forced her to sit as tight against him as she could and wrap her arms around him. She held on tight with her good hand and hooked the ends of her casted fingers into his pocket with her bad hand.

All the bikers she knew really well were riding with them, along with a couple she didn't. When they all started their bikes the ground shook, and she loved it.

Steele turned his head and yelled, "make sure you hold tight Little Mouse." She leaned in closer and then got caught up in the smell of him. "Are you sniffing me?" He questioned.

She shook her head no, then promptly continued to sniff him. He chuckled and called her a nut. Then he lifted the kickstand and roared out of the parking lot. She screamed and forget all about sniffing him.

She loved the ride and wanted nothing more to throw out her arms and pretend she was flying. The bikes were in a tight formation and they surrounded her. All then men looked so powerful and intimidating. She wanted to do this every day.

Suddenly, from out of nowhere came two black escalates. They were still ten minutes from the station. Steele yelled at her to hold on as he cranked the bike faster. She clung to him as the escalades got closer. She watched in confusion as Trike broke formation, speeding off ahead of them.

All the bikers pulled out their guns and started firing. She heard Preacher yell to shoot at their tires. She desperately wanted to close her eyes, but knew that wasn't a good idea. Bullets flew all around her, and then one of the escalades skidded and immediately flipped over, barely missing Navaho.

She screamed as a bullet whizzed past her head, then Dagger was there, putting his bike between Ryker's bike and the vehicle. Tears streamed down her face as she realized these men would die for her.

She watched in terror as the car tried to hit the back of Dragon's bike. But, Dragon had seen him coming and sped up, swerving out of the way at the last second. The escalade was still focused on Dragon, and she watched as Navaho moved up and quickly shot the driver. He slumped in his seat, and the man in the passenger seat tried to grab the wheel. It was no use, the vehicle swerved off the road and crashed into a tree.

She sagged against Ryker as she saw the police station ahead of them. About a dozen officers were out front with guns, Trike standing beside them.

Chapter Twenty Four
Steele

Steele swerved into the police station with his brothers on his tail. The officers moved to the side, but stood guard as they all set their kickstands down and dismounted. When he turned to look at his Little Mouse, she had tears streaming down her face and she was trembling. He moved right to her and pulled her into his chest.

"Dragon almost got hit by the escalade. Dagger put himself between me and the bullets. You all got shot at," she blubbered. He scooped her off the hog and shoved her face into his neck. He just kept repeating, "it's all right, I've got you," over and over to her. He had no idea if she heard him though.

Preacher pointed to the station, silently telling him to get her inside. He headed for the door, and an officer held it open for him. He was led down the hall to a huge conference room. He picked the closest chair and sat, still trying to soothe her.

Slowly the room began to fill with bikers and two detectives. Nobody said anything, they waited silently for Cassie to pull herself together. Another five minutes and she did. She wiped her eyes, she sucked in a breath and she sat up straighter in his lap, but she didn't get off!

Preacher immediately started yelling. "What the fuck was that," he roared.

Without missing a beat, one of the officers explained. "Those were Mario's men."

Everyone at the table froze. Steele knew Mario. He was the local loan shark, and he was tough. If you owed him money, you were in serious trouble.

"What the fuck does that have to do with us or Cassie," he questioned. He barely contained his rage, but he knew he'd find an outlet soon!

"Apparently, Cassie's husband Parker, owes him a ton of cash. He's cleaned out his accounts and jumped ship, but Mario still wants his money. As Cassie's still married to him, the debt falls to her."

The whole room erupted at once. Bikers yelled, and the detectives yelled back. Finally fed up, Preacher wolf whistled to get everyone's attention.

One of the detectives stepped forward. "We know Parker's in serious trouble, and we know Cassie is innocent. We've found the cops that were working with him, and they're being dealt with. You won't have any more trouble with them. We've got eyes on the streets and we're trying to get information about the loan. We also have every available man looking for Parker. We'll find him." The detective paused then and faced Cassie.

"We need to get you into protective custody immediately," he told her.

Steele wrapped his arms around her and held tight. "No fucking way," he roared. "We have the manpower, and we have the compound, she stays with us." His brothers growled in agreement.

Cassie bravely faced the detectives. "I'm not leaving Ryker," she said. "And his brothers just put themselves in front of bullets for me. Right now, I trust them completely. I don't trust you," she told them.

"Okay," they agreed. "But you keep in touch with us, and you watch your backs. You run into any trouble, you call us. You hear from Parker you call us."

"We hear from Parker, we definitely will not be calling you," Preacher told him. Then the detectives and Preacher had a stare down.

Preacher must have won because the detective looked to the ceiling and muttered, "I don't want to know."

Steele smirked and set Cassie on her feet. "Let's go," he commanded the bikers. As one they stood and headed for the door. "You wanna ride back with me, or you want me to put you in a cage," he asked his Little Mouse.

"I ride with you," she told him. Then she stood on her tippy toes and kissed him. He growled and kissed her back. Then he put her on the back of his bike and took her home.

Chapter Twenty Five
Cassie

The ride back to the compound was quiet. Cassie clung to Ryker as he powered the bike down the country ride. She leaned her head on his back and sighed. Things were getting steadily out of control, and she had no idea how to fix them. She felt Ryker momentarily squeeze her thigh in support. No matter what, she knew he would be there for her.

They leaned right and left as they rode down the winding road. She leaned with him, completely in tune with his movements. She loved being on the bike with him. It was a freedom she had never experienced before.

She really wished she had met him years ago, how different her life could have been.

When they got close to the compound, she felt Ryker slow the bike. She lifted her head to look over his shoulder and froze. In front of the gates were six escalades and a limo. In front of them stood about two dozen men, and all of them had guns. Ryker immediately braked as did the other bikers. Their bikes skid on the gravel before coming to a stop.

One of the men moved to the limo and opened the back door. A handsome man dressed in a very expensive looking suit stepped out. Cassie stared at him as Ryker pulled his gun and aimed it at the man.

The man held up his hand as he spoke, "there's no need for bloodshed today. I take it you know who I am," he questioned.

"Mario," Ryker growled. He broadened his body as he flicked the kickstand down, and instantly she was blocked from view.

"You are protective of the girl, I admire that," he said. "However, I'm here to offer you a deal. Parker owes me five million dollars." He looked the bikers in the eye, "I want my money, or I want Parker."

Cassie gripped Ryker's arm and held on. "Ryker," she whispered. When he tilted his head back, but kept his eyes on Mario she told him, "Parker should have that much money, that's what he cleaned out of all the accounts."

Ryker's back went straight, and he shot out. "According to his ex-wife he cleaned out their accounts and has that much money with him."

"Ah," Mario said. "With him though is not with me." He took a step towards the bike and as he did all the bikers turned their guns on him. "Come now, you know what happens when the bullets starts flying. I lose men, you loose men, and chances are the girl will get hit. I know you don't care about yourselves, but I bet that girl means something to all of you."

Cassie trembled, and she moved to lean over Ryker's shoulder again. "I don't want anybody hurt," she told them all.

Mario smiled, "and there's my sweet girl. How about you climb off that bike and come with me? You can be my guest for a week while your bikers locate Parker for me. When the week is up, you get to go home and I get my money. Now how does that sound," he asked.

"No fucking way," Ryker roared.

"Now my sweet girl, would like to see these men die?" Mario looked at her as he waited for her answer. She shook her head no.

"I didn't think so," he replied smugly. "Give your biker a kiss goodbye and come to me."

Cassie grabbed Ryker's shoulders and hopped down. He immediately grabbed her around the waist and crushed her to him. "Stay with me," he demanded.

"I can't lose you," she told him. "Find Parker and bring me home," she pleaded. Then she kissed him quickly and wiggled out of his arms, hurrying to Mario. As Mario took her hand and helped her on the limo, the last thing she heard before the door shut was Ryker's cry of rage.

Chapter Twenty Six
Cassie

Cassie sat in the limo as far away from Mario as she could get. She leaned her head against the window and let the tears fall. He didn't try to talk to her, and she was grateful for that. All she wanted was Ryker. She just wanted him to hold her. She was tired of being afraid. She was tired of being hurt. She was tired of being unloved.

She noticed the limo start to slow and realized they were pulling up to a huge house. The house was two stories and there were pillars out the front. She saw a fountain off to the side and a massive four car garage sat beside it.

The limo came to a stop, and the door was opened.

Mario stepped out, then leaned down and offered her his hand. She slowly scooted over and placed her hand in his. Once she was out, he let go, but placed her arm in the crook of his, then he headed to the front door. A guard opened the door and Mario escorted her inside.

There was a grand staircase inside, and Mario headed right for it. Up they went until they hit the second floor. He led her down the hall, then stopped at a door. He released her and pushed open the door, motioning her forward.

The room was stunning. It had a four poster bed, an antique dresser and mirror, and there was a window seat for reading. She could even see a huge master bath off to the side. Her shoulders slumped, all she wanted was to get away from the money, and here it was staring her right in the face yet again.

"Do you not like it," she heard Mario ask.

"It's beautiful," she told him truthfully.

"The closet is stocked, please help yourself to anything. My room is across the hall if you need anything please do not hesitate to ask. There is a full library at the end of the hall, please help yourself to anything in it. Supper is in about twenty minutes. I will leave you, but I will be back then to escort you." With that he turned and left, shutting the door behind him.

Cassie moved to the window seat and slumped down. The gardens were immaculate, but she didn't see them. She pictured Ryker's face, and closed her eyes for a minute, just wanting to forget everything for a little while.

She awoke to a light hand shaking her shoulder. Mario was leaning down studying her. "Let's get some supper into you Pretty Girl. While we eat, we can talk. I need you to feel comfortable here, and I need you to trust me. No harm will come to you while you are in my home."

She wasn't sure what to make of that, but when he offered his arm, she placed her hand on it and let him lead her from the room. She was curious, as instead of heading downstairs to where she knew the formal dining room would be, he headed in the direction of the library. The doors were already open, so they went right in.

Off to the side was s small table set up with their dinner. It sat in front of a huge window which again faced the lavish gardens. He led her to it and pulled out her chair. She said nothing as she sat down and watched him take the seat opposite her.

"I hope you like fettuccine," he said. "I noticed you have a cast, so I wanted a meal you could eat easily. I need to know though, was it Parker that hurt you, or was it someone else."

She sat quietly for a minute, then lifted her head and told him it was Parker.

"As I thought Pretty Girl," he smiled at her then. "You and me are going to get along just fine. You can rest here and heal, you are only here to motivate your biker, nothing more. At the end of the week, regardless of whether he finds Parker, you are both free to go."

He then turned to his food and dug in. She stared at him a minute, full of questions, but his slight nod to the food had her digging in as well.

Chapter Twenty Seven
Steele

Steele paced the clubhouse. His Little Mouse had been gone nearly four days now, and they still had no leads on where Parker was. Every brother had been pulled in and finding Parker was their only concern now. Every day half the club took to the streets, searching houses, asking questions and threatening anyone that may know him. Favours were called in, and markers were collected, but still no Parker.

Steele was worried about his Little Mouse. Mario was known for his brutality, and after everything that had happened to Cassie, he had no idea what frame of mind she would be in when he got her back. He couldn't even think of the possibility of not getting her back. That wasn't even an option.

Another group of brothers rode in, and Steele met them to see if they had anything. Dagger was the first to greet him, slapping him on the back and bumping shoulders.

"You know, you don't shave soon, you're gonna scare your girl when she sees you. You have been showering right," his brother asked.

Steele just growled, and the biker lifted his hands in surrender. "Okay, too soon, got ya. So there have been no more visits to the bank, and he hasn't been back to his house. Still no sign of his car. Trike checked the bus and train stations, and no one matching his description bought a ticket. Fuckers still here somewhere, but he's dug in deep. I got another group of brothers checking every abandoned building from here to the next town, and we are checking all the woods for any sign of camping gear, although with what I've heard of Parker, he isn't the camping type. My take is, wherever he is, he still has his luxuries."

Steele nodded, agreeing one hundred percent. "Thanks brother," he rumbled. "Navaho put on a spread, eat, rest and I'll see you in a bit."

"Will do," Dagger agreed. "We'll get him brother, your girl will be home soon." Then he turned and headed into the clubhouse. Steele stood there for a few minutes, then turned to his hog, cranked it, and tore off down the road.

Soon he was pulling into the long driveway of Cassie and Parker's house. He powered down his hog, flipped the kickstand and headed inside. Everything was quiet, and it pissed him off. He needed a fight, something, anything to release some of the tension in his body.

He pushed open the front door and headed up the massive staircase. He turned to the room his Little Mouse used and moved inside. The house made him uncomfortable, but this room calmed him. It was all her, it was softer and not so expensive looking. He was beginning to understand Cassie's reaction to the money. He was starting to see that she didn't want any of it, and it thrilled him.

He sat on the bed as his cell buzzed. He ripped it from his pocket and checked the screen, an unknown number.

"Steele," he growled.

For a minute there was nothing, and then he heard it, "Ryker."

"Little Mouse," he roared sitting up straighter. "How did you get a phone?"

"Mario let me use his," she told him. "I wanted you to know that I'm okay. He hasn't hurt me and he's been really nice. I don't want you worrying about me."

"I'll always worry about you Cassie," he told her. "But I'm fucking thrilled to hear your voice. I'm glad you're doing good, but I still want you to know, you're mine. In four more days, regardless of whether I have Parker, I'm coming for you, and I don't care what I have to go through to get you back. You'll be on the back of my bike and in my bed that night. I love you Cassie," he whispered.

"I love you too, Ryker. I'll see you in four days," she told him.

"Four days," he swore, then hung up smiling for the first time in days.

Chapter Twenty Eight
Cassie

Cassie hated being away from Ryder, but Mario was easy to be around. He made her feel relaxed and at ease. She had free reign of his house and grounds and as long as she didn't leave the property, none of the guards even paid attention to her. She loved taking a blanket and just sitting in the flower beds.

That's where she found herself now, curled up on a blanket enjoying the sun. She loved the smells coming from the flowers, and all the different colours made her feel happier. She could just sit, without any worries. She really wished Ryker could join her though, then laughed at the image of her big biker sitting in a flower garden.

She heard movement from behind her and turned to see Mario approaching. He had a basket in his hand and a smile on his face.

"Hello Pretty Girl, I brought lunch, if you'd let me join you," he asked. She sat up and moved over, making room for him on the blanket. He took her silence as acceptance and sat beside her, placing the basket between them. He looked out of place in his designer suit, but he didn't seem to care.

He proceeded to spread out grapes, strawberries, cheeses and crackers. "I figured a nice lazy lunch would be fun, and this seemed like picnic fare."

She smiled at him and admitted, "it's perfect." Then she grabbed a grape and popped it in her mouth. She looked up at him, studying him for a few minutes. He really was a handsome man, but she only had eyes for Ryker.

"You love him don't you," he asked. "It's okay, if you don't feel that way about me, I understand. I can't say I'm not disappointed though. You're a beautiful woman with so much to give. He's a lucky man."

She smiled at him. "He's come into my life when I need him the most. He shows me a love like I've never felt before. I feel safe with him, and I've never had that before. Even just looking at him that first time, I felt a connection. He's all I can see now," she whispered.

Mario smiled at her. "You amaze me. Parker was incredibly abusive towards you." He took her casted wrist in his hand and kissed her fingers. "Even with all that, he didn't break you. You can still love and have a healthy relationship."

"Ryker makes me stronger," she told him honestly. "Without him, I wouldn't have had the courage to leave. He makes me want more."

"What about your parents", he inquired. "How do they feel about all this?"

She looked to her lap before answering. "My parents know about the abuse and told me I just need to be a better wife. They want grandchildren at any cost to me. They even signed over my inheritance to Parker. He has more than enough money to pay you." She told him.

"Do they show you any affection," he quietly asked.

She shook her head sadly. "They didn't want a daughter. You can't pass down a company to a female. That's why they dote on Parker so much. He's like a son to them."

She sat back then, stunned, as she thought about what she said. "He's like a son to them," she repeated. Thoughts ran through her mind, one after the other.

"My parents love Parker," she stated.

"Cassie, what is it?" Mario's concerned gaze was on her alertly.

She smiled huge at him. "Can I use your phone again for a minute," she pleaded.

"Anything for you," he said. Then he shifted to his hip and pulled his cell out of his back pocket. With a tender look, he took her good hand in his and placed the cell in her palm. She closed her hands around it.

"I think this is the end of our time together," she told him. Then she hit the button that would connect her to her heart.

Chapter Twenty Nine
Steele

Steele bowed his head, all but defeated. He had two more days to go before the deadline was up and he was all out of options. He stood at the bar in the clubhouse and drained his beer, then he turned and threw it at the wall. The empty bottle smashed against the concrete, and he felt no different. He had hoped it would release some tension, but it only made him want to throw another one!

His brothers were tired. As soon as they came back in from a search, he gave them time to eat, then he sent them back out again. They scoured the three neighbouring towns and still had no leads. Parker had effectively disappeared off the face of the earth. They pretty much knew he hadn't left town, but they had no idea where the hell he went.

Dagger came up next to him and clapped him on the shoulder. "Prospect," he bellowed. Seconds later a prospect came running in from the kitchen. "Clean that shit up," he ordered him as he pointed to the mess on the floor. The prospect nodded and headed in that direction.

Dagger turned his full attention to Steele, so Steele faced him and waited. "We still have two days brother," he pushed. "The fucker's gonna screw up and we got brothers everywhere."

"And if he doesn't," Steele muttered.

"Then we mount up with our pieces and storm the castle. We bring your girl home either way brother." Dagger eyed him dangerously until finally Steele nodded. Then he leaned over the bar, grabbed two more bottles and popped the tops. Steele took the bottle Dagger held out and tipped it back, draining half the bottle in one pull.

Navaho came in then and unhooked his tool belt, dropping it on the nearest table. Then he made his way over to the bar and grabbed himself a beer. Steele tipped his chin in his direction in a silent greeting.

"Outside is completely finished," Navaho explained. "I'm done the wiring and plumbing and have just started to drywall the inside. Painting should start late tomorrow afternoon. By the end of next week I should have the cabinets and fixtures in and it should be about done."

"Brother," Steele mumbled. "Appreciated." Then he hung his head and admitted, " I just hope my Little Mouse will get to see it."

"Fucking right she will," Navaho growled. "Maybe we should start messing with Parker's shit. You know, break shit at his house, trash the law firm, petty shit that they can't pin on us, but that will hopefully draw him out."

Steele thought about it for a minute. "That's not a bad idea. Pull shit kids would do, so it looks like it was teenagers. Do a little B and E.

I think the whole club would be down for a bit of fun."

Trike wandered over then. "I'm really good at blowing shit up," he volunteered. Steele raised his brows at his newest brother in question. "Used to work with explosives a lot when I worked for a road crew, a while back. Kind of still dabble in it for shits and giggles," Trike admitted.

Steele shook his head and laughed, but did so saying, "I'm not sure we should go that far yet, but I like that line of thinking." Then he grabbed a beer for Trike and handed it to him.

"Who's up for a bit of mayhem," he roared. He laughed when everyone of his brothers present roared back at him. They all had a new spark in their eyes, as if things had just been way to boring now, and Steele had offered them a way to fix that.

He could only sigh as his phone rang. Everyone was fired up and ready to roll, but one look at the screen had him hitting the button to answer it.

Chapter Thirty
Steele

Steele put the cell up to his ear and closed his eyes. "Little Mouse," he questioned.

"Ryker," his Cassie called enthusiastically. "What are up to," she asked.

He smirked, "getting ready to do a little B and E, possibly blow some shit up." He waited as there was silence on the other end of the line.

"I think you need to explain that," she whispered. "I'm not sure how blowing things up will help," she whispered in his ear.

"Boosts moral," he told her. "Spirits are low and the brothers are tired, it's kind of like a pep rally for bikers," he explained.

He heard Cassie giggle on the other end of the phone and he smiled. At least in the worst of times his girl could see the humour in things. Cassie always amazed him.

"Right," she said. "But maybe you won't need to go that far. Me and Mario were talking, and it got me thinking." She paused then, and he gritted his teeth at the thought of Mario chatting to his girl.

"Has anyone thought to check out my parents place," she asked.

Steele stood in silence for a minute, then roared, "god damn," as he screamed at his brothers to mount up. Bodies instantly sprang into action as his brothers sensed his sudden tension and jumped to do as he asked.

"Love you Little Mouse," he groaned. "Now I gotta let you go, so I can finish this," he told her as he made his way out the door after his brothers.

"I love you too," she signed as she hung up. He jammed his phone back in his pocket and made his way to his hog.

With the questioning looks his brothers were giving him, he bellowed miserably, "fuckers probably at her parents, and has been all along. I can't believe I didn't think to check there. Her god damned parents dote on him and don't give a shit about Cassie," he told them.

Navaho was by his side in an instant, but he turned to Trike as he said, "boy, bring that dynamite anyway, no reason we can't still stir a little shit and have some fucking fun doing it." Then he grinned at Steele and made his way to his bike. Steele laughed evilly as he powered up his hog. Then he flipped the kickstand back and roared out of the compound with at least fifteen bikes following him.

Twenty minutes later they parked at the end of her parents street and were hoofing it through the trees behind their property. Cassie's parents were pretty isolated as they lived in a huge fucking house at the end of the street. Thankfully there weren't many neighbours as the houses were ridiculously far apart.

His brothers moved pretty quietly for a bunch of huge men wearing shit kickers, and in minutes they were behind the house. Navaho immediately left the group and silently disappeared to check out the house. Ten minutes later he returned, explaining the parents didn't look like they were home, but Parker was curled up on the couch watching tv.

Steele smiled at that, this was gonna be fun. His brothers looked on in anticipation as Steele quickly surveyed the house. It was massive, with a garage off to the side, a pool in the back and a glassed in sun room off the kitchen. He spotted the patio furniture and came up with a plan.

"Dagger, Navaho and me will be back in a minute. The rest of you wait here until we get back." Then he motioned for his brothers to follow him. When they hit the patio he said, "as quietly as you can get all the patio furniture in the pool."

Not one word was spoken as the brothers did what he asked without question. Then they slipped back to where the rest of them were waiting. He grinned and turned to Trike. "You got that dynamite," he asked.

Trike outright laughed as he pulled tons of it out of a knapsack. "I got more than enough brother," he told him as he practically bounced on his knees in excitement. Next, he pulled out a lighter and things got interesting.

Chapter Thirty One
Steele

Steele couldn't help but feel his adrenalin spike as he held the lighter to the stick of dynamite Trike had in his hand. He knew he should feel some sort of guilt for what he was about to do, but he couldn't sum any up. Cassie's parents were assholes, and that just made this so much better.

He lit the fuse and told Trike to throw it right in the middle of the pool. Trike smiled and stood up. After taking careful aim, he lobbed it high in the air so it came down directly in the middle of the pool. All his brothers hunkered down and covered their ears, but all their eyes remained unwaveringly focused on the dynamite.

Trike's aim was true, and he didn't disappoint one fucking bit. The boom of the dynamite going off was deafening, but it was what happened after that kept the brothers attention. Patio furniture shot out of the pool like rockets. Some of it smashed on the concrete around the pool while others shot through the glass sunroom breaking the entire structure and sending glass flying in every direction.

Then the tidal wave hit as all the water in the pool flew into the air and came crashing to the ground. What was left of the sunroom was crushed under the weight of the water. Then they watched in silence as the diving board flew through the air and embedded itself in the side of the garage. Everything went silent for a second, then it happened.

Parker came flying out a side door and stood paralyzed as he surveyed the wreckage of a backyard. He glanced about, of course looking for the attackers. When he couldn't see anyone, he turned and made a bee line for the garage.

Suddenly, a stick of dynamite flew through the air and Steele watched as it landed on the garage, blowing it to bits. He turned to Trike, and his brother shrugged as he smiled. "Anticipation," he told him unapologetically. Steele looked around as his brothers roared with laughter.

As Parker slowly turned around, abandoning the garage Steele couldn't help but laugh with his brothers. Parker was covered in wood chips, and for once he didn't look put together. His hair was a mess and his shirt was untucked, not to mention he was only in socks. As a group, all his brothers stood at once.

Parker glanced in the direction of the bikers and turned a deathly shade of white, then they watched in disgust as he pissed himself.

"Why do they always do that," Dagger muttered.

Parker instantly ran, and the bikers cursed as they all gave chase. He was no match for fifteen angry bikers and they took him down in seconds.

"Christ he stinks," Navaho complained. He motioned to the two prospects, and they moved forward to haul him to his feet. The man was sobbing and had snot running down his face.

Steele got close to him and growled, "act like a fucking man." That only made Parker start to struggle and try to pull out of the hold the prospects had on him.

"Jesus I don't want piss on me," one of the prospects griped. Steele didn't blame him, and moved quickly, slamming his fist into the man's face and instantly knocking him out. The prospects immediately let out a breathe in relief.

Steele started bellowing instructions. "Prospects, get that fucker in the van and make sure nobody sees you. The rest of us will be there in fifteen." The prospects nodded and headed off back through the woods, dragging Parker behind them.

"The rest of you pick up all traces of the dynamite you can find, we can't afford to leave any of it behind. Dagger, can you set up a gas leak so the house goes up and covers this up," he asked his brother.

Dagger smiled. "Give me ten minutes. When I come back out of the house you better be done because it will blow pretty quick."

Steele smirked," perfect, let's get shit done," he roared as his brothers moved into action, all acting like happy little kids. Man they needed more days like this he thought.

Chapter Thirty Two
Cassie

Cassie handed back the phone to Mario with a smile on her face. She prayed Parker was at her parents, because that meant this was almost over, and she really needed this to be over. She wanted Parker to be in the past because she knew without a doubt that Ryker was her future.

She could finally dream about being happy and the possibility of having children. She always wanted kids, but she refused to even think of having a child with Parker. She didn't want someone so precious to her suffering at his hands.

She could close her eyes and picture a little boy that looked just like Ryker. Or, a sweet little girl that Ryker would dote on and adore. She grinned even more at that thought. Ryker would go ballistic if anyone threatened his little girl.

She looked over at Mario who was looking at her curiously. "That's a pretty big smile," he grinned back at her.

"Ryker's headed to my parents, and I'm praying that Parker's there. I was just thinking that today could be the day I get to finally put him behind me. I need some happiness in my life."

Mario looked horrified. "And you haven't been happy here with me? I've been bending over backwards to make sure you enjoy your stay here." She would have been sad that she upset him, but then he smiled again, easing her worry.

"I'm sorry, but my happiness now belongs to Ryker. I just need to be with him," she sighed.

Mario took her hand. "Things are going to work out for you," he told her. "Now, how about we go sit on the front porch and wait? It could be a bit before we see or hear from your biker, but it's a beautiful day, and I think you want to be in the perfect spot to watch him arrive."

She nodded enthusiastically at him. "That would be perfect." Mario helped her up, and together they made their way around the house. When they were comfortably seated, they continued to chat about nothing until about two hours later when the ground shook with the rumble of motorcycles approaching.

Cassie jumped from her seat and ran down the steps, standing at the bottom and straining to catch a glimpse of the bikes. A few minutes later and she was bouncing with nerves as she finally saw them approaching. Of course, Ryker was in the lead.

The minute he shut down the motorcycle she flew towards him. He barely had time to drop the kickstand and step off the beast before she reached him. As soon as she got close, she launched herself at him and he had to take a step back as he caught her. She heard his laughter as he hugged her tighter against his chest. She wrapped her legs around him and clung.

"When you leave, I'm going with you," she all but cried.

"You bet your ass you are," he growled back. Then he took her chin in one hand, making sure he still had a firm hold on her, and tilted her face up. Her heart fluttered as he lowered his head and pressed his warm lips against hers. She immediately opened for him and his tongue surged inside.

Hoots and catcalls forced them apart, but she needed a breath anyway. She looked up at him with stars in her eyes as he walked her to the porch where Mario stood waiting.

He stared the man down as he lowered her carefully to her feet. As she tried to step away, Ryker grabbed her around the waist and pulled her flush against his body.

"I've gone almost a week without touching you, don't you dare think of leaving my side," he growled. She loved it when he wanted her closer, so she instantly tucked herself into his side.

"I have Parker," he told Mario.

Chapter Thirty Three
Steele

Steele was over the moon to have his Little Mouse back in his arms. She was just as soft and sweet as he remembered, and he loved the way she curled into him. They were gonna have a future together, he could guarantee that.

He didn't take his eyes off Mario. The man had been kind to Cassie, but that didn't mean he trusted him. Mario had her by his side for almost a week, and that was time he didn't get with her, so he was on edge.

Mario was glancing back and forth between him and Cassie, and he got the feeling he was being judged. When Mario turned away and looked towards the other bikers, Steele figured he got his approval, and that just pissed him off.

Finally, Mario started things moving, "I don't see Parker." He then turned back to Steele and raised his eyebrow.

Steele gave a shrill whistle, and Dagger moved to the van that was parked behind all the bikes and threw the side doors open. Two prospects jumped out and dragged Parker out of the van behind them. He was fully conscious, but didn't seem to be fighting. Steele waved the prospects towards them.

When the prospects got close enough they stopped. He could feel Cassie tense up beside him, so he tightened his hold on her, trying to silently reassure her. She relaxed slightly in his arms. Parker however, turned his attention on her and stared.

Steele kicked his leg to get his attention and growled, "you don't get to look at her anymore asshole. Eyes anywhere but on her." Parker grunted but looked away from his girl.

Mario immediately raised his hand and snapped his fingers, gaining Parker's eyes. "Where's my money," he asked.

"Safe," was all Parker hissed.

"Hm," Mario started. "If you don't tell me where right now, I think I'll give you to the bikers. I hear one of the brothers, Dragon I think, likes to torture people with a blow torch." He turned to Steele then, "am I correct," he asked.

Steele smirked at him, "yeah, you're correct," he admitted sadistically.

He turned to Parker, who had visibly paled and begged him, "please don't tell him where the money is. We need to let off some steam, and I have a new knife I want to try out."

Parker seemed to twitch for a minute, then he yanked his right arm free and ripped the prospects gun from the back of his pants. He shoved the second prospect away and grabbed Cassie's shirt front, yanking her against his chest. Quickly he spun her around, so her back was to his front and used her as a shield.

"Mother fucker," Steele growled. Then, he raised his hands in a gesture of surrender and motioned towards Cassie. "Let her go asshole."

Steele looked around, all his brothers had their pieces out and they were all aimed for Parker. "Take it easy brothers," he ordered. "I don't want Cassie hit."

Cassie had instantly started crying and was twisting, trying to get free. Steele watched in shock as Parker raised the gun and aimed it at him. "She's mine," Parker roared as he pulled the trigger.

Cassie screamed as the bullet tore through his side. The pain was excruciating, and he fell to his knees. Cassie was sobbing and tears were streaming down her face as she tried to free herself and reach him, but Parker refused to let her go.

Navaho came over and knelt down, putting his hands over the wound. Steele cursed as the pressure caused the pain to increase. He looked up at Cassie and tried to smile at her. "I'm okay Little Mouse," he said soothingly.

All he could do then, was kneel helplessly and watch as Parker dragged Cassie away. His brothers wouldn't shoot and risk hitting her. She screamed and cried out for him and it broke his heart. Parker dragged her to the van and forced her in, then Steele watched as they tore away.

He roared in anguish as his brothers surrounded him waiting to hear what he wanted them to do.

Chapter Thirty Four
Cassie

Cassie fought hard to keep calm. Her worst nightmare was coming true, Parker had her again. She thought this was over, but she had been so wrong. He had shot Ryker and then dragged her away. She had no idea if he was okay, and that was killing her. She had a pain in her chest, and it wouldn't go away.

Ryker had done so much for her in the last few weeks, and now he was left with a gun shot wound to his side. It was all her fault. If she never would have met him, this never would have happened. He was possibly dying, and it was all because he had met her.

She turned to look at Parker and saw he was furious. His face was almost red he was so mad, and his mouth was pressed tight together. She had no idea what he was capable of now, but she knew she was in serious trouble. If she didn't get away, he could really hurt her.

Slowly, she leaned towards the door. He glanced at her for a second, then turned back to face the road, completely ignoring her. She reached up and grasped the door handle. Giving it a quick twist, she threw the door open and turned in her seat, ready to jump.

As she pushed off, Parker reached out and grabbed her hair, yanking as hard as he could. Cassie was wrenched back into the van, and her leg slammed into the door. She cried out in pain.

Immediately, Parker stomped on the brakes, jerking the van to the side of the road. She reached back, scratching and tearing at the arm that held her hair. Parker forced the van into park and turned fully towards her in the seat. Because she was still facing the door, when he yanked her head down she found herself lying in his lap.

She stared up at his hard expression and sobbed.

"Please let me go," she begged him.

She saw no sympathy in his expression, and it terrified her. He leaned down and kissed her brutally. She cried out as he bit her lip and she tasted blood. He wrenched her head up, and spun her around in the seat, then punched her in the side of the face.

She slumped down in her seat, dazed from the blow, while he reached across her and slammed her door shut. The locks clicked as he hit them, permanently sealing her in. He glared at her a minute before turning away and throwing the van back in drive. She could only whimper as he pulled back out onto the road.

Ten minutes later they pulled up to her parents house. She was horrified as she stared out the window at the sight in front of her. The house was just gone. Police and fire trucks lined the drive, and it was a flurry of activity. Even though the site was devastating, she couldn't find it in her to feel sorry for her parents. They had been awful to her, and she thought of the saying, what goes around comes around.

Parker cursed beside her, and then drove past the house. She watched him as he left their street and drove to the next one. He finally stopped at the house directly behind her parents.

He threw open his door and climbed out, grabbing her arm and hauling across the seats and out behind him. When she was standing beside him, he slammed the door shut and then pulled the gun out of his pocket. She felt a slight burn as he jammed it into her side.

"One word, or you try to fight me and I'll do to you what I did to the biker trash," he hissed.

Tears sprang to her eyes as she thought of Ryker.

"Fuck it," he rasped. Then he moved quickly and hit her in the head with the butt of the gun. She didn't even have time to cry out because everything suddenly went black.

Chapter Thirty Five
Steele

Steele bellowed out in rage. He was on Mario's porch lying on his side, with his brothers hovering over him. Navaho was currently stitching the hole in his side back together and fuck it hurt. He didn't want his side stitched, he wanted to go after Cassie, but his brothers wouldn't let him up.

"This is gonna get fucking infected if you don't let me finish," Navaho roared. "Five minutes and we can go after your girl. You're damn lucky the bullet just grazed you. Fucker is a terrible shot," he told him.

Terrible shot or not, it still fucking burned, but Steele didn't care. As long as he could stand and ride, he was good to go. Navaho tied a knot and cut the thread, then Dagger held his shoulders, anticipating him getting up.

"Let him cover it," Dagger barked. It only took Navaho a minute longer to slap on some gauze and tape.

"You'll probably tear your stitches, but for now you're good to go," Navaho told him.

Steele shrugged off Daggers hands and stood. Preacher held out his cut to him that Navaho had made him take off. He figured he could patch the hole, but he didn't know if he could get all the blood out. He shrugged and pulled on the cut.

"When did you get here," he questioned Preacher.

"Long enough to listen to you wine as you got the stitches," Preacher growled. "Trike followed the van. Parker parked on the street behind Cassie's parents. He headed in on foot and he had your girl over his shoulder. He can't go far with all the cops around, so I figure he's only there to grab the money. He must have hidden it somewhere on the property. Once he gets it, he'll probably bug out, so we need to move fast."

Steele immediately nodded and moved towards his bike. His brothers followed closely behind.

"You got this, or do want some back up," Mario asked.

Steele started his hog as he turned back to the man. "I got this," he growled. "We'll be back with the money if we find it, but you won't be seeing Parker again," he promised.

Mario raised his hands in surrender, "that's all I need," he agreed.

Steele turned to face the road and flipped the kickstand, then they all pulled out. He couldn't wait to get his hands on Parker. He was gonna reign hell on the bastard.

Ten minutes later and they pulled up behind Trike's bike and the van on the side of the street. He quickly pulled out his cell and punched the button to call Trike. He answered on the first ring.

Trike immediately spoke, not even waiting for a greeting, "head through the yard and jump the fence at the back. Walk directly through the trees. After a second, you'll come to an old well on the back of the property. Parker's hauling up a bucket now and it looks like the bag of money's inside. Cassie's sitting beside the well and he's got a gun pointed at her head. I can't risk taking him out myself in case he hurts her. You only have a minute before he's probably gonna take off again."

Steele hit a button and shoved the phone back in his pocket. He stomped across the yard and headed for the back, with his brothers right behind him. He was pretty sure he pulled a couple of his stitches out jumping the fence, but then he was off again, barreling through the woods.

Finally, he saw Trike and moved in his brothers direction. Trike put his finger over his mouth, telling him to be quiet, then he pointed off to the side. Steele turned in that direction and watched in horror as Parker picked up Cassie and attempted to throw her in the well.

All stealth tactics were thrown out the window as Steele roared and tore out of the woods.

Chapter Thirty Six
Cassie

Cassie was terrified. Parker had absolutely lost it. She had woken up on his shoulder. The bouncing as he walked was killing her stomach. She knew they were cutting through the neighbours yard towards the back of her parents' house, but she had no idea why. With all the police around, she had no idea what he was thinking.

She screamed as Parker threw her over a fence, and she hit the dirt on the other side. She couldn't get up fast enough before he had jumped the fence to land beside her. He immediately grabbed her hair and dragged her along behind him.

She lost a shoe and felt a sting on her leg from a branch that tore through her jeans. She grabbed at his hands and scratched at his arm, but he wouldn't let go. Finally, he stopped and reached down, hauling her to her feet. He grabbed her arm and twisted it back. She cried out as her shoulder popped and she knew he had dislocated it.

The pain was excruciating, but he wrapped his arm around her waist and they were off again. He was practically carrying her again as black spots danced in front of her eyes. She was thankful when he stopped and threw her to the ground. She carefully sat up and took a look around.

They were still in the woods at the back of her parents' property. But, Parker had stopped at the old well. She knew they were way too far for any of the police to see or hear them, so she knew she was on her own.

When she tried to stand, Parker shoved her back down and held a gun against the side of her head. "Move, and I'll blow your fucking head off," he hissed.

Cassie held perfectly still, trembling because she knew he had meant every word. She watched in silence as he grabbed the chain for the bucket in the well and began hauling it up. It took him awhile, as he only had one hand, but she could tell he almost had it to the top.

He glanced down at her and smirked as the bucket breached the opening. She watched as he reached over and grabbed a duffle bag from inside the bucket and pulled it out. He tossed it to the ground beside her, and then let the chain go. The chain made a horrible squeaking sound as it unraveled and then she cringed at the splash the bucket made as it hit the water at the bottom.

With the gun still at her head, she looked over to watch as he opened the bag and peered inside. She gasped as she saw huge bundles of money lying inside. She assumed this was the money he had taken out of the bank that was owed to Mario. Somehow though, she knew he didn't plan on giving any of it to him. He was going to run, of that she had no doubt.

He smiled down at her and she was suddenly terrified. He moved the gun away from her head and shoved it down the back of her pants. She tried desperately to scramble away, but her arm hampered her, and he laughed as he grabbed her hair again to haul her to her feet.

She had no time to react as he picked her up and threw her towards the opening of the well. She tried to grab on to him, but she couldn't get a good hold, and then it was too late. She screamed as she hit the side and then tumbled to the bottom. She landed in the water and cried out as her head went under.

In desperation, she grabbed for the bucket and pulled her head out of the water. With all the strength she had left, she wrapped her good arm around the chain and held on.

She screamed and sobbed as she realized how bad a situation she was in, but then she heard it. A deafening roar sounded from above ground, and she knew Ryker had arrived. Now all she had to do was hold on just a little bit longer.

Chapter Thirty Seven
Steele

Steele lunged for his Little Mouse, but he was too late. His heart broke as he heard her screaming on the way down. Finally, there was a splash, and he knew she had reached the bottom. He prayed the water wasn't too deep.

He bellowed as he grabbed Parker by the neck and threw the man to his brothers. Then he was at the well and leaning as far as he could onto it. He felt a hand grabbing the back of his jeans, but he ignored it. His Cassie was far below, but he could hear her crying and screaming his name.

He roared her name, and she instantly quieted.

"Grab the bucket Little Mouse and I'll put you up," he shouted down to her.

He waited a minute as he couldn't see her, and when he hoped he had given her enough time, he gripped the chain and started to pull. Instantly, Dagger and Navaho were at his side, grabbing where they could and straining to help.

They only pulled for a minute before they felt the weight leave and heard a splash. They stumbled back as the bucket flew up. Steele shoved himself to his feet and grabbed the side of the well to peer down.

"Cassie," he roared. He could hear splashing, but he couldn't see her.

Suddenly, the bucket went flying over his shoulder as Dagger threw it back down the well. A few seconds later the splashing stopped as she grabbed hold of the bucket again. Steele was dying inside imagining the terror she must be feeling.

Preacher came up to him then and shoved a flashlight in his hands. He nodded to his prez, then flicked it on and aimed it down into the hole. His heart stopped as he got his first look at his Little Mouse.

Cassie looked like she was soaked, and she had blood on her cheek. She held on to the bucket with only one arm, and the other hung limply at her side. She looked tired and in pain, and he didn't know how long she'd be able to hold on. He had no idea how deep the well was, but he knew he didn't have much time.

"She can't hold on," he roared desperately. Trike pushed him out of the way and took the flashlight out of his hand, then his brother leaned over the side and peered down. After a minute, he turned back to Steele.

"I'm the smallest brother here," he told them. "I'm still a big guy, but I bet if I can climb down that chain, there should be enough room for me to get a hold of her. But, then it's gonna take almost every brother here to pull us up, and I can only pray that chain holds my weight. It's the only way I can see to help your girl," he told Steele.

Steele didn't waste any time. He nodded to Trike gratefully and took the flashlight back. In an instant Trike was over the side and carefully reaching in to grab the rope. Steele grabbed his arm and helped lower his brother into the well. When he was sure Trike had a good hold on the chain, he let go. Dagger, Navaho and Preacher crowded around him to peer down the well in concern.

Trike wrapped his feet around the chain and slowly lowered himself hand over hand. It was a painfully long few minutes, and the chain was slick, causing him to slip a couple times. Steele was paralyzed with fear as he imagined his brother falling and landing on Cassie. It took almost ten minutes for his brother to reach the bucket, and Steele let out the breath he was holding when he did.

The easy part was over, but Trike still had to reach down and get a hold of his girl. This was turning out to be the worst day of Steele's life.

Chapter Thirty Eight
Cassie

Cassie saw someone climb into the well way above her. Unfortunately, she couldn't tell who it was. She was too far down to hear anything, and it was so bright at the top that all she could make out was a black figure at the top. She was getting extremely cold and tired, and she didn't know how long she could continue to hold the bucket. She was shivering and her arm was shaking, but with the water being so deep she knew that if she let go, she'd die.

She leaned her head against the bucket and turned so she could look up. The person was slowly making his way down the chain, but it would be awhile before he reached her. She hoped it was Steele, but the figure just didn't look big enough.

She had cried so much and screamed so loud that her throat was raw. She knew Steele was at the top, and she wished with everything she had that she could just hear his voice. She needed so badly for him to hold her. She knew everything would be fine if she could just curl up in his arms.

The figure was about halfway down now, but he was so large that he was starting to block out all the light. She was terrified that soon she would be thrust into darkness, and then when she couldn't hold on she would just sink to the bottom of the well. She didn't want to die. She really wanted a chance to be with Ryker.

The figure was almost to her now, and he angled his head so he could see down to where she was hanging. It was then she realized it was Trike who was making his way down the chain. She whispered his name, but she didn't think he heard her.

As he reached her, he placed one of his feet in the metal bucket she had her good arm wrapped around. Instantly, his weight was too much, and the bucket was ripped from the chain. Cassie screamed at she fell into the water, along with the bucket. Then she was pushed further down as Trike's weight landed on top of her.

She kicked hard, trying to move around him and reach the surface. She felt a hand on the back of her shirt, and it ripped a bit, but Trike had a good hold of it, and she was dragged up beside his body. She gasped in air as her head broke the surface.

Trike wrapped his arms around her as he kept both their heads out of the water. She was weak, but she managed to wrap her good arm around his neck.

"Trike," she whispered again.

"I got you sweetheart," he promised. "And, I'm not letting you go." Then he looked up to the chain and reached up grabbing it and holding tight. "Wrap your legs around me, and hold on tight," he instructed.

Once she had wrapped herself around him as best she could, he placed a soft kiss on her head. Then he raised his head and roared "pull" to whoever was at the top.

It took a minute, but slowly she felt them rising. She cried softly as her emotions suddenly went haywire. Her arm was in extreme pain now, and it hung limply at her side. She knew she was in trouble as her strength started to leave her. She panicked as her arms and legs loosened, and she started to fall.

She had no idea how Trike managed, but he let go with one arm and wrapped his arm around her chest, holding her just under her arms. She found herself staring at his stomach. Somehow, he was now only holding on with one arm.

"Pull faster," he bellowed. "I'm loosing her."

Immediately, the speed doubled and she could hear the grunts of the bikers at the top. It sounded like the whole club was up there. She sobbed in relief as Trike reached the top and hands grabbed him to pull him out.

Then Steele was there, taking her from Trike and lifting her over the side. She clung to him, praying this was the last time they were separated. She loved him, and again he had come to her rescue. He was cementing his place in her heart and she couldn't be more grateful for the day he came into her life.

Chapter Thirty Nine
Steele

Steele finally had his Little Mouse in his arms. She was soaked to the bone and shivering, but she was alive. He couldn't seem to hold her tight enough, and even though he was afraid he was hurting her, he just couldn't seem to loosen his hold. She was crying, and she seemed to be holding him just as tight.

He held her as long as he could and then looked up to lock eyes with Trike. He put everything he could into his expression in thanks, his brother would always have his gratitude. He knew he would never be able to repay him for what he had just done. Trike nodded his head in acknowledgment and then let Preacher lead him away.

Dagger came up to him then and clapped him on the back. "Let's move brother," he ordered. Without a word, Steele scooped up Cassie, and then followed his brothers back through the trees. He knew the cops weren't far away, still trying to comb through the wreckage of Cassie's parents' house. Things would go south fast if they were discovered.

He stomped through the woods furious at Parker, but excited about finally getting his revenge. The fucker had done enough damage, it was time for him to do some of his own.

When Steele got to the fence, Trike was waiting on the other side. He had to pry Cassie's cold fingers from his neck, and he could feel her panicking. Once she noticed they were at the fence, and saw Trike with his arms out, she relaxed and let him go. It took everything he had, to actually hand her to his brother, but he knew it would be next to impossible to get over the fence with her.

In one giant leap he was over and reaching for her again. Trike understood and wasted no time handing her back over. Again, her cold little arms wrapped around his neck and she clung to him. It only took him a few minutes to cross through the neighbours yard and reach their hogs.

He stopped cold when he got a look at everyone waiting. Dragon and Ali were standing there, along with his brothers, but he was surprised to see Mario and a some of his men waiting as well. He ignored him and headed straight for Dragon.

"Brother," Dragon greeted him. "I brought a blanket for your girl." Immediately, he helped Steele wrap it around Cassie. She burrowed into it and laid her head on his shoulder. "You're gonna ride back with Ali in the truck, and I got your hog. I got doc waiting at the compound, so all should be good. Mario and his men have offered to escort Parker to the clubhouse, seeing as we cut both the prospects loose. Those fuckers messed up, they aren't Iron Brotherhood material. We've already given Mario the bag of cash, so everything's taken care of."

Steele turned to watch as Mario's men took a messed up looking Parker off of Navaho and Dagger and threw him in the back of the van. This time, the man was hog-tied, and several others jumped in the back with him. The door slammed shut and the rest of Mario's men made their way to a couple cars. Mario raised his hand in acknowledgment, then climbed in the back of one.

Steele turned back to Dragon, grateful to his brother for getting everything taken care of. Ali's hand on his arm drew his attention to her. He didn't have anything else to worry about, so he followed her to Dragon's truck. His Little Mouse needed medical attention and probably a warm shower, and that was what he would concentrate on getting done for the moment.

Parker was being taken care of, and he wasn't getting away again. Soon though, his Cassie would sleep, and when her pretty eyes closed, Steele would head to the shed. He had some pain to dish out, and it wasn't going to be pretty. Parker would die tonight, and he would do it slowly.

Chapter Forty
Steele

Steele was so proud of his Little Mouse. He knew she was extremely tired, and he knew she had to be in quite a bit of pain, but she was up and trying to follow him. He smiled at her as he looked down at her clothes. He loved seeing her in his shirt and boxers, but he didn't want his brothers to see that much skin. The shirt was so big on her, that it practically hid the boxers completely.

Steele routed through his dresser and came up with a pair of sweatpants that had a drawstring. She watched him skeptically, but he just smirked. He crouched down, and she immediately put her hand on his shoulder. He quickly stripped her of the boxers and helped her get on his sweats. Then, he had to laugh at the sight of her. He must have rolled the legs up six times, and he rolled the waistband down twice. She looked ridiculous, but at least she was covered. Ali had only bought Cassie a couple pairs of jeans, so Steele would rectify that tomorrow.

He picked up her bat and took her hand with his free one, leading her out of the room. When he hit the common room, Dragon, Trike, Dagger and Preacher were waiting. They raised their eyebrows at the site of his Little Mouse trailing along behind him. He smirked at them, and they just shrugged.

He scooped her up, causing her to squeal, and followed his brothers out the door and across the compound. When they reached the shed, Preacher banged on the door. Navaho opened it and peered out at them. After he made sure it was them, he opened it wide so they could make their way inside.

He still held Cassie and watched as she looked around curiously. She noticed the tools laid out on a bench and paled slightly, but then her eyes hit Parker, and she seemed to gain her strength back. She wiggled in his arms, so he carefully set her down.

He watched as she tore her eyes from her husbands and turned to Trike. His brother stared at her silently for a minute, and then his eyes widened as she crossed the shed and threw herself into his arms. Steele balled his hands into fists and stayed where he was, as his Little Mouse cried in his brothers arms, and whispered her thanks. Trike just held her and let her cry.

Finally Steele figured he had been patient enough, so he stomped to them and pulled Cassie from Trike's arms.

Trike turned to him and said, "I know, I know, I'll get a beating for that later."

When Steele just continued to glare, he felt his Little Mouse's fist connect with his shoulder. He looked down, to see her scowling up at him, and he heard chuckles from his brothers. He turned to them and demanded that they just get started. They nodded in agreement, and everyone turned their attention to Parker.

Parker was hanging from chains in the ceiling, with his arms pulled high above his head. He was wide awake and staring at Cassie. Steele was surprised to see anger on the man's face. Most men that were brought in here, were pale and begging at this point.

"Well darling," the asshole said. "It looks like you've finally hit bottom. You're seriously going to side with garbage."

His Little Mouse straightened her shoulders and moved closer to the man. Steele and his brothers all became alert as they kept their eyes on her, ready to step in if they had to.

"You raped me," she whispered. "You hurt me," she continued. "You took vows promising to love and protect me, and you never gave me that."

Then she turned away from Parker and headed for him. It broke his heart to see the tears in her eyes. Without a word he passed her the bat. She held it awkwardly in her left hand and headed back to Parker. Steele followed, just in case she needed him.

His brothers all watched in fascination as she reared back and brought it down on Parkers dick. She didn't have a lot of force behind the blow, but her aim had been true. They cringed as Parker howled in pain. Cassie then walked up to him and spit in his face.

She turned back to Steele and handed him the bat, then she stood on her tiptoes offering him her lips. He pulled her close and kissed her deeply. Then he passed her to Trike and watched as he took her arm and led her away.

Now the fun could really start.

Chapter Forty One
Steele

Steele stood in front of Parker and stared at him. He could tell he was still in pain from Cassie's blow, and he was happy about that.

"Your woman has some spunk in her," Preacher stated. "I like her."

"You stole my wife," Parker growled.

Steele eyed Parker for a minute. "You lost her a long time ago," he told the man. "That girl is mine now, and things are gonna change for her. I cherish and protect what is mine. That means I'm gonna spend every day of my life making sure she's loved and that she never knows so much as a paper cut again. Your loss is my gain fucker."

"You'll never get away with killing me, people will be looking for me," Parker yelled.

Steele and his brothers smirked at the man. Then Dagger stepped forward. "I blew up Cassie's parents' house earlier today. That means it will take days to comb through all that rubble. We can basically do anything we want to you, and then we just burn part of your body. If we sneak in tonight and bury it in the debris, then the cops will figure you died in the explosion."

Parked paled, and it looked like he started to sweat. Steele slapped Dagger on the back. "Works for me," he said.

Finally, Parker broke down. He pleaded and begged and even shed a few tears. Steele had absolutely no sympathy for the man. He turned to Dragon, "I really like using my knife, but I think this would be the perfect opportunity to get a lesson with the blowtorch. I watched how you used it on the prez of The Outlaws after they took Ali, and I was impressed. And, since we're going to burn him anyway, what difference does it make?"

Parker started to shake, and then he pissed himself. "God damn," Navaho said. "That's twice in one day, what the hell kind of man are you, anyway?"

Dragon snored as he headed to the tool bench for his blowtorch. Steele watched Parker slowly lose it as Dragon turned on the torch and warmed it up. After a minute, he headed back over.

"Now, you should probably wear my visor as it gets pretty messy. There's really no way to go wrong, except if you get too close to something vital, then you'll kill him pretty quick. I suggest you play for a while, then burn something important. We can't dump the fucker with a bullet in his head."

Steele nodded in agreement, then grabbed the visor and pulled it over his face. Next, he took the heated blowtorch and turned to Parker smiling. The man was outright screaming now, and Steele could only laugh at him. He slowly got closer, drawing it out. Parker twisted in the chains, trying to move away.

Steele raised the torch and burned a line down the inside of his arm. Parker screamed louder and then passed out. "What the hell," Steele said. Suddenly, Navaho came up beside and threw a full bucket of cold water at the man. Parker sputtered and coughed, but at least he was awake again.

Steele took his time then, and forty-five minutes later he was ready to end him. He had burned almost all of Parkers body, but the burns were just to the surface. Navaho had gone through about twelve buckets of water. Steele brought the torch to Parker's head and pushed it close. Not even ten seconds later, Parker was dead.

"I enjoyed that," Steele said as he handed the blowtorch back to Dragon. "But from now on, I'm sticking with my knife. I have to say, I really don't like the smell," he told his brother.

Navaho and Dagger stepped forward then. "Go take a shower," Dagger told him. "Your girl's a widow now, so you're in the clear to claim her. We'll clean this up and take him over to the house. It's late, so it should be no problem to slip in. We won't hide him too well that way he'll get discovered faster."

Steele gave all his brothers a slap on the back and a one armed hug, then headed inside to his girl. Finally, their life together could begin, and he couldn't fucking wait.

Chapter Forty Two
Cassie

Cassie woke when the bed shifted. She rolled over and found herself face to face with Ryker. He smiled at her and pushed the hair off her face. Then he leaned in and gave her a soft long kiss on the cheek. She melted against him, mindful of her arm, and kissed him back. She was disappointed when he pulled back and sighed.

"A couple more days Little Mouse, then there will be no reason for us to stop," he told her. "I need to claim you officially, but I don't want to do that until everything's behind us. I'm content right now to hold you and have you close."

"He's gone then," she asked, not wanting to say his name while in bed with Ryker.

Ryker nodded, and she moved as close to him as she could get. He wrapped his huge arms around her and she basked in his warm, strong body. She was happy, she thought as she fell asleep, she'd never felt that before.

She woke the next morning and found she was practically on top of Ryker. She realized he was already awake. "How long have you been awake," she whispered.

"Bout an hour," he shrugged. "I just wanted to watch you sleep for a while. There's nothing I need to do this morning. Want me to help you cleanup, then we can get some breakfast," he asked.

She nodded in agreement, then giggled as he lifted them both out of the bed and headed for the bathroom. He helped her shower and get dressed, then he brushed her hair. She loved how careful and attentive he was towards her. When he was done, she turned around to face him.

"I love you," she told him quietly. When he went to speak she placed her finger over his lips. "I just want you to know that I've never said that to anyone else. I cared about Parker in the beginning, but neither of us ever said the words." She looked away then. "I don't remember my parents saying it, and I know I never said it to them." She stared at him as a tear fell down her cheek.

Ryker brushed the tear away and studied her for a minute. She began to get nervous and went to turn her head away. He caught her chin and stopped her from moving.

"I love you with everything I am. You mean absolutely the world to me. I promise to protect you, to make sure you have everything you could ever need, and to tell you everyday I'm breathing that I love you. There will never be a day that goes by that I don't tell you that. You deserve to hear it all the time, and I'm happy as fuck that I get to be the one that tells you," he growled.

The tears fell furiously now as she threw herself into his arms. They stood there for a long time without moving, just enjoying each other. Finally, her stomach growled and Ryker laughed, turning and pulling her out the door and towards the common room.

She was surprised to see a lot of bikers already there. Navaho immediately pointed towards a table and Ryker led her towards it. But, instead of pulling out a chair for her, he sat and pulled her onto his lap. Then, Navaho was there placing two heaping plates in front of them.

Somehow Ryker ate and helped her eat at the same time. She was slightly embarrassed, but he seemed completely happy, even giving her quick kisses every so often. Preacher gave him grief about it, but he just raised his middle finger, then ignored him.

They had just finished eating when Dagger called Preacher to tell him cops were at the front gate. Cassie's stomach rolled as she panicked. She was falling in love with all the bikers and she didn't want anyone in trouble because of her.

Ryker stood and pulled her up with him, heading for the door. She turned at a loud noise and was shocked to see every biker in the clubhouse rising as well and following them out. She now knew the meaning of the word family.

Chapter Forty Three
Steele

Steele tucked his Little Mouse into his side as he stood at the gate, facing the two detectives. He was flanked by most of his brothers, and he was thrilled to see the support they offered Cassie.

The two detectives just happened to be the two from the station that had helped Cassie previously. They immediately approached and addressed him.

"We have some news for Cassie," one of the detectives said. "Do you want to do this with an audience?"

Steele turned towards Cassie and raised his brow in question. "Yes," she whispered. "I don't mind them hearing whatever you have to say."

"Fair enough," he replied. "It looks like there was a gas leak in your parents house yesterday. The explosion took out the entire house. We discovered that your parents were at a conference and luckily weren't home at the time. We have contacted them, and they are on their way back now."

The detective turned to face all the bikers. "Would any of you know anything about that?"

Preacher stepped forward. "Are you insinuating we had something to do with that," he growled.

The detective raised his hands. "No I am not," he declared. "But I have to ask, for my report." Preacher nodded in acceptance.

The detective then turned back to Cassie. "I'm afraid I have some bad news," he smirked.

Steele knew that when they were at the police station, the detectives were furious at the way Parker had treated his Little Mouse. He figured they were just as happy as he was the asshole was dead.

"I'm afraid your husbands body was discovered among the wreckage. While we were out searching for him, your parents were hiding him. I'm sorry Cassie," he told her.

Cassie nodded. "So what happens now," she asked.

Steele pulled her closer as the detective answered. "Nothing. We had to use dental records to identify him, so we don't need you. We've made some inquiries, and as his sole survivor you get everything, or at least what he didn't clean out. The house is yours, and he had a substantial life insurance policy that's now yours. You need to decide what to do with his ashes as he was cremated. The body was too damaged to do anything else," he smirked.

Cassie turned to him and looked up at him smiling. "It's over then," she said.

"No Little Mouse," he said. "It's just beginning." Then he kissed her softly. He never heard the detectives say their goodbyes and leave.

Ten minutes later they were back inside the common room with all the bikers. Even Dragon and Ali were inside. Steele turned to Dagger and nodded his head, indicating it was time. Dagger immediately got up and headed to the back. He came back a second later with a box, setting it on the table beside him.

Steele turned to Cassie and pulled her close, getting her attention. "Little Mouse, I know I'm not the type of man you pictured yourself with. I'm a biker, I'm loud, I'm kind of rough around the edges, but I'll love and protect you until the day I die. I wonder if you'd do me the honour of wearing my patch and becoming my old lady. I promise, it will be a life full of adventure, and you'll get a huge overprotective family."

His heart melted when she nodded, and silent tears streamed down her face. He turned to the box and pulled out the vest he had made just for her. The patch on the front said Little Mouse, and the back said Property of Steele. He carefully helped her get her good arm in, then he draped it over the arm in a sling.

Immediately, his brothers erupted into cheers and then some of them came up, pounding him on the back in congratulations. After a couple brothers leaned in and kissed Cassie, he'd had enough.

"Fucking bikers," he muttered as he pushed them out of the way and picked up his Little Mouse, carrying her out of the room. Their life was beginning and there was no way in hell he was starting it with his brothers watching.

Epilogue

Cassie curled into Ryker as they laid in bed. It had been almost a month since Parker's death, and she couldn't be happier. For a couple days it had been stressful. Cassie had refused to collect Parker's remains. She had no idea what would happened to them, but Steele told her they would probably be picked up by his parents. Of course, he was right.

Two days later, her parents showed up at the gate. When Ryker and his closest brothers went with her to the gate, she was overwhelmed with the support. It was going to take her a while to get used to the affection and support they continuously showed her, but she was loving it.

Her parents were appalled by Ryker and made their opinions known. Then they demanded that she attend her husband's funeral. If that wasn't enough, they told her about their house, and explained she needed to give them hers as payment for raising her.

She calmly explained that Ryker was the man she was going to spend her life with. She told them there was no way in hell she was going to the funeral for a man that threw her down a well and tried to kill her. Then she explained that they were now on their own, and that there was no way she was supporting them, when they refused to support her when the beating were happening.

Her parents were outraged and screaming while she herself pulled the gate closed and walked away. She had never felt better. It was a huge weight lifted off her shoulders, and she planned to never see them again.

Ryker had surprised her with a cabin on the back of the property, looking out over a lake. It was absolutely beautiful. He was so nervous showing her as he knew it wasn't what she was used to. She had cried, telling him how perfect it was. She didn't want a big, cold house. She wanted a small, cozy home. He was relieved and had proceeded to drag her into the cabin to show her how much.

They made love for two days solid after that, and when they got hungry Ryker would call up to the clubhouse, and food was quietly left on the porch for them. Ryker, of course, had furnished the cabin, but he forgot to stock it with groceries.

They talked about marriage, but decided to wait a year. Cassie loved Ryker, and didn't plan on ever leaving him, but she just wanted a bit of time to pass first. Ryker was okay with that, but he set the wedding date for exactly one year later! She had no arguments and readily agreed.

Cassie had sold her house and gave the money to the club. She specified that she wanted it used for bikers that fell in love, but couldn't afford to put up cabins of their own. She had lived in the clubhouse for a while, and even though she loved all the bikers, she needed her privacy. She wanted others to get that same peace of mind.

Ryker and her had only fallen deeper in love. They were happy in their cabin, and Cassie had found a best friend in Ali. Ali was due any day now, and she and Ryker had been named godparents. A couple days ago, she had stopped her birth control, and now they were trying to make a baby of their own.

As Ryker had promised, things were never boring, and there was always someone around to lend a helping hand. Her life had changed for the better, and even though she had to go through something terrible to get here, she wouldn't have wished it any other way. She was now a biker chick, and she was damn proud of it.

About the Author

MEGAN FALL is a mother of three who helps her husband run his construction business. She has been writing all her life, but with a push from her daughter, started publishing. It's the best thing she ever did. When she's not writing, you can find her at the beach. She loves searching for rocks, sea glass, driftwood and fossils. She believes in ghosts, collects ridiculous amounts of plants, and rides on the back of her hubby's motorcycle.

MEGAN FALL

Look for these books coming soon!

STONE KNIGHTS MC SERIES
Finding Ali
Saving Cassie
Loving Misty
Rescuing Tiffany
Guarding Alexandria
Protecting Fable
Surviving November
Sheltering Macy
Defending Zoe

DEVILS SOLDIERS MC SERIES
Resisting Diesel
Surviving Hawk

THE ENFORCER SERIES
The Enforcer
The Enforcers Revenge

Loving Misty
Stone Knight's Book 3

Chapter One
Trike

Misty carefully lifted her hand and felt across the top of the bathroom counter. Finally, she located her brush. Picking it up, she ran it through her long golden brown hair. She loved her hair, as it was the same colour as her mothers, and wished with everything she had that she could see it now.

Almost two years ago, she was driving to dinner with her parents. An impaired driver crossed the median and hit their car head on. Both her parents were killed instantly. She suffered quite a few cuts and bruises, but the most damage she received was to her head.

The back of her head slammed into the side window from the impact. The doctors told her she had significantly damaged the optical cortex. It caused her to suffer a partial blindness, meaning she is only able to see shadows and shapes.

The blow also caused headaches and dizzy spells. The doctors told her that there is no indication of how long the blindness could last. For some people it last days, others months or a year, and in some cases it never returns at all.

For her, she figured it was permanent. She still suffered the headaches and dizziness, only not as often, but since the accident, her sight hadn't improved at all. She was just as bad off now as she was when it happened.

She sometimes wished she was completely blind. The shadows only frustrated her and made it harder. The light hurt her eyes too, so she had taken to wearing sunglasses when she was out during the day.

Her brother Noah was a marine and been stationed in Afghanistan at the time. He was given leave to come home and attend the funeral. He also stayed long enough to make sure she was settled, then he was under orders to go back. He had to sell her parents house, to pay for the funerals and her medical bills, so he had moved her into his apartment. Since he was engaged to Carly, and she was their only family, Misty was now in her care.

Unfortunately, as soon as Noah left, Carly showed her true colours. She hated being Misty's caregiver and was constantly making it known. Plus, Misty was pretty sure Carly was seeing someone else behind her brothers back. Her brother only called about once or twice a month, and with him stationed in the middle of a battlefield, Misty knew she couldn't burden him with her problems. She put up with Carly's abuse and went on with her life.

Most days she sat at home and read on the Braille book reader her brother had bought her. She also liked to pop in her ear buds and listen to music on her iPod. Sometimes she ventured to the park down the street, but even that was difficult.

Today, Carly insisted on driving her to a coffee shop, and she planned on leaving her there while she went to run a couple errands. She promised she would only be about forty-five minutes, then she would pick her up and take her back home. Misty didn't really want to go, but she knew she needed to start getting out more.

That's why she had been searching for her hairbrush. She kept begging Carly not to move her things, but of course Carly told her she needed to clean, and to do that she had to put things away. Sometimes it took Misty an hour to find her things after Carly cleaned. It was frustrating and some days she even shed a few tears. Misty knew Carly did it on purpose, just to upset her.

Misty finished in the bathroom, and grabbed her cane, heading out to the livingroom in search of Carly. She finally found her waiting by the door as Carly liked to ignore her when she called. Misty sighed and followed her out of the apartment and downstairs to her car. She was careful on the stairs as Carly never helped. Once they had made it to the car, she opened the door and climbed in.

She hoped her afternoon was better, but didn't have very high hopes. Life just wasn't what she expected it to be anymore, and she was beginning to lose hope of it ever getting better.

CPSIA information can be obtained
at www.ICGtesting.com
Printed in the USA
FFHW02n1021280918
48618270-52561FF